D0870822

Also by J.A. Lang

Chef Maurice and a Spot of Truffle (Book 1)

CHEF MAURICE
AND THE
WRATH OF GRAPES

J.A. Lang

WITHDRAWN FROM
RAPIDES PARISH LIBRARY

PURPLE
PANDA
PRESS

RAPIDES PARISH LIBRARY
ALEXANDRIA, LOUISIANA BK

Paperback edition published by Purple Panda Press

Copyright © J.A. Lang 2015

J.A. Lang has asserted her right under the Copyright, Designs and Patents Act 1988 to be identified as the author of this work.

All rights reserved. No part of this publication may be reproduced, stored or introduced into a retrieval system, or transmitted, in any form or by any means, without the prior written permission of both the copyright holder and the publisher.

ISBN 978 1 910679 05 0

This book is a work of fiction. Names, characters, businesses, organizations, places and events are either the product of the author's imagination or are used fictitiously. Any resemblance to actual persons, living or dead, events or locales is entirely coincidental.

To Dad

CHAPTER 1

Chef Maurice, head chef and owner of Le Cochon Rouge, the finest and only restaurant in the little Cotswold village of Beakley, currently found himself stuck between a rock and a hard place.

The rock in question was the smooth stone wall of the restaurant's wine cellar, which was pressed up against his back and was, in the typical manner of many a solid stone wall, refusing to budge.

The hard place was a large bottle of vintage Champagne, which, as he'd squeezed his way past, had been dislodged from its slumbering position on the tall shelving unit opposite. Already on its side, the bottle had begun a gradual heart-stopping roll towards the edge of the shelf— a trajectory that would have spelt bubbly disaster if Chef Maurice hadn't possessed the presence of mind to quickly stop it in its path.

Unfortunately, while he possessed the necessary presence of mind and quick-fire reactions honed by many decades in professional kitchens, he was currently experiencing a lack in the available hands department, as both his own were already engaged in clutching three bottles of wine apiece.

The height of the shelf, at eye level, had also discouraged the use of an enterprising knee or handy elbow.

So he'd used his nose.

It was a good nose, large and prominently placed, and supported by a moustache of walrus-like proportion.

Thus, man and bottle had reached a tentative equilibrium.

From the sounds above, dinner service was just wrapping up, the frantic buzz of the kitchen slowly descending into the gentle hum of leisurely dessert orders and postprandial coffees.

At some point in the not-so-distant future, someone was bound to notice the gaping hole left in the staffing, and come looking for him.

Hopefully, this would occur fairly soon, as the Champagne bottle was thick with dust from many years of storage, and he could feel a sneeze coming on any minute now.

Footsteps sounded at the top of the cellar stairs.

"Everything all right down there, chef? We're all waiting for you to start."

Thank goodness for Patrick, his ever-reliable sous-chef.

"*Oui*, all is good. But I perhaps require your assistance for one moment . . ."

Patrick reached the bottom of the steps, conducted a speedy assessment of the situation, then, sighing, walked over and grabbed the dusty bottle, and set it back to its usual place.

"I did mention last week it's getting a bit crowded down here," he said, as Chef Maurice flicked the dust out of his moustache. "And it's not just our inventory. I reckon we're using at least a third of our shelves for storing customers' own bottles for them. Maybe it's time to consider charging a small f—"

"Bah! Our most loyal customers come here to eat because they know they can leave with us a special bottle or two, to enjoy at the correct moment. It is therefore our pleasure to host their wines."

"*Oui*, chef. But maybe we should at least think about rearranging the shelving and—" Patrick stopped as he caught sight of the half-dozen wine bottles in Chef Maurice's hands. "We're drinking *all* of those tonight?"

"Tasting," called a voice from the top of the cellar stairs. It was Arthur Wordington-Smythe—Chef Maurice's best friend, sharp-nibbed food critic for the *England Observer*, and the somewhat reluctant Chair of the newly formed Cochon Rouge Wine Appreciation Society.

"It's called a wine *tasting* for a reason," Arthur reminded them. "Tonight is all about learning, not drinking."

"Hmph," said Chef Maurice, who had a deep suspicion of drinkers who spent more time swirling, sniffing and slurping than good old swallowing. "Wine is not to be learnt at a desk. It must be lived!"

"And, ideally, remembered the following morning," said

Arthur. "Anyway, Maurice, this tasting was your idea in the first place."

That was true enough. Mandatory wine training for the restaurant's staff had come about via an unfortunate incident involving a rather expensive bottle of Barolo. Chef Maurice, following a favoured customer's request, had brought the bottle upstairs to the kitchens to sit upright for a few days, to give time for the wine's grainy sediment to settle down into the base. Unfortunately, this had also given time for Alf, the restaurant's young commis chef, to mistake the bottle for part of a sauce recipe, pull the cork and empty the contents into a hissing saucepan.

Everyone had agreed it was the best red wine jus they'd ever served with a herb-crusted rack of lamb, but probably not the most financially viable addition to the menu.

Alf had been close to tears, and Chef Maurice had been forced to surrender a fine old bottle of Burgundy from his personal collection to appease the bottle's owner (who had, thankfully, been rather gracious about the whole matter, especially after tasting the superlative lamb).

Still, it at least presented an opportunity to instigate a few sessions of wine education, in the hope of decanting a little vinous knowledge into Le Cochon Rouge's kitchen crew.

Patrick and Alf were already seated in the dining room at a square table covered in a forest of wine glasses. Dorothy, the restaurant's long-time head waitress, was still bustling back and forth across the floor, tending to the evening's remaining diners.

Arthur took his place at the head of the table, giving them all a solemn nod. "Evening, gentlemen. Thank you for your attendance at this inaugural meeting of the Cochon Rouge Wine Appreciation Society. Maurice has asked me to lead the proceedings, while he has prepared a selection of samples for the food-and-wine-matching portion of the evening."

Chef Maurice nodded from his seat behind a wide tray, which held a pile of sliced tomatoes, a steamed sea bass, two pan-fried duck breasts, a tub of sardines in olive oil, a multitude of cheeses, and a large slice of chocolate cake.

"Tonight we'll be tasting three whites and three reds," continued Arthur, "as well as introducing the elementary techniques of wine tasting. Let us begin."

He picked up the first bottle, encased in a dark cotton bag to obscure its label, and trickled a sample into each of their glasses.

"Anyone know where we start?"

"By drinking," said Chef Maurice promptly, downing his glass and reaching for the bottle.

"No," said Arthur, moving the bottle out of the chef's reach. "Anyone else?"

"Smelling?" volunteered Alf.

"Almost. First, we begin with observation. You'll notice a white napkin in front of you. Hold the glass up in front of it, tilting it like this, just so, and tell me what you think about the colour."

"It's yellow," said Alf, peering into his glass.

"Indeed. And what type of yellow?"

"Weeellll . . . " Alf scratched his ear. He was a gangly lad in his late teens, and had joined the team at Le Cochon Rouge in a bid to learn all about, as he put it, 'haughty cuisine'. "Reminds me of the time we had too much asparagus in the kitchens, and chef let me take a whole bunch home for dinner, and later that night—"

"Yes, thank you, Alf, I think we see where you're going with that," said Arthur hurriedly, "but a simple description of 'greenish-yellow'—"

"—more like yellow mixed with pea green, as in—"

"—would have sufficed at this stage."

Alf looked over at Patrick, who shrugged.

"Next," said Arthur, raising his glass to his nose, "we study the aroma. First *without* swirling"—he looked pointedly at Alf, who was whirling his glass around on the table like a fairground teacup ride—"then afterwards with swirling. We do this because aerating the wine by swirling the glass releases a whole new set of aromas."

"Mmm. Citrussy," said Patrick, nose in glass. "Bit of grass, too."

"Very good," said Arthur, nodding encouragingly. "I get a distinct hint of lemon zest. Though, of course, wine is always a very personal experience."

"That is very true," said Chef Maurice, who was himself enjoying a personal experience with his third glass.

Alf, not to be outdone, took another deep sniff. "All I can smell is grapes," he complained.

"Excellent!" said Arthur. "This grape variety is known to have a particular aroma of fresh grapes."

"If that's so, then my bet is on a nice fresh Muscadet," boomed a voice from behind Arthur.

"*Non, non,* for you, this is too easy," said Chef Maurice, turning to waggle a friendly finger at the newcomer. "They must learn for themselves. But come, join us. You have met my staff before, *n'est-ce pas?* Patrick, Alf, this is Sir William Burton-Trent. His home is the big house over the fields there." He waved his glass in the general direction of the kitchens.

"You own Bourne Hall?" said Alf.

"That's the one," said Sir William. "It's a grand old pile, though sadly getting on in years. As am I, though at least I haven't quite reached my third century yet, even if a young chap like you might not believe it!"

"This man," said Arthur, nodding at the towering Sir William, "has one of the finest private cellars in the whole of England."

"And it's full of wine too," added Sir William with a hearty wink. "Rather too full, in my mind. But once you get on this collecting lark, I'm afraid drinking the stuff has to take a back seat sometimes."

"That is not a problem I have found," said Chef Maurice, slicing off a chunk of brie from the tray in front of him.

"Good man! Wine's made to be drunk, keep telling myself that. But when you're there at auction, and a pretty

7

little half-case of Mouton comes up, straight from the chateau itself, well, you've got to be a stronger man than I to resist, I tell you."

He clapped Chef Maurice on the back, causing the chef to drop his cheese.

"Speaking of Bordeaux," continued Sir William, "I'm having a little party tomorrow evening, nothing fancy, just a dinner and tasting. Bordeaux versus California—my own take on the Judgement of Paris, you might say. If you and Arthur don't have anything on, you're more than welcome to stop by. And Meryl, of course," he added, nodding at Arthur.

"I'm afraid she's off at a conference, but I'm sure she'd have been delighted—"

"To hear us old bores go on about vintages and soil and minerality and all the rest of it, I'm sure," said Sir William with a chuckle. "Righty-ho, I'd better let you get back to your tasting. Never forget, *in vino veritas.*"

His face took on a dark expression. "Hah, or so I thought . . . " he muttered under his breath as he turned away.

"What was that he said?" asked Patrick, watching Sir William stride out of the front door.

"It's Latin for 'in wine there is truth'," said Arthur.

"Is there truth in wine?" asked Alf, sniffing at his glass.

"*Oui*, the truth of a good drink!" Chef Maurice raised his glass in toast.

"And what was that he said about judging Paris?"

"The Judgement of Paris," said Arthur, pouring out the next wine. "It was a competition between France and California in the 1970s to see who produced the world's so-called best wines. The judges were all French and the wines were tasted blind, no labels. The Californians won, and the French went off with their noses in slings."

"Bah, that is what happens when you let an Englishman do the organisation," said Chef Maurice, shaking his head. "Now, enough talk, we must concentrate on the wine."

"Sure thing, chef," said Patrick, grinning.

Wine Tasting 101 continued apace. Patrick discovered a partiality to the Rieslings of the Mosel region. Alf discovered that Chilean Cabernet Sauvignon did not pair well with tomatoes, sardines, nor chocolate cake.

And far away, down in the dark of the Bourne Hall cellars, far from the clink of glasses in Le Cochon Rouge's dining room and the sound of Alf gargling with tap water, there was the gentle scrape of glass on glass as a heavy bottle was slowly removed . . .

CHAPTER 2

It was a frosty December evening. A sprinkling of snow danced down through the yellow lamplight in the gravelled backyard of Le Cochon Rouge.

"They say we might get a blizzard tonight," said Arthur, as he swung the car out into the narrow country lane.

Chef Maurice grunted from behind his thick woolly scarf. He was not a fan of snow, especially when it was heavy enough to keep his customers huddled up at home instead of out eating in his restaurant.

"If this carries on a few more weeks, we might even be in for a white Christmas."

"Hmph."

Even after several decades in the country, Chef Maurice had yet to fathom the Englishman's near fanatical interest in the state of the weather. A gust of wind, a few drops of rain, and every man and woman was a sudden meteorologist, holding forth about isobars, pressure gradient forces, and Arctic wind patterns.

Perhaps, he thought, it was some modern form of

weather worship, in case talking incessantly about the level of cloud cover might one day cajole the Weather Gods into bestowing a Mediterranean climate upon the gloomy British Isles.

"So who do you suppose will be at tonight's soirée?" said Arthur.

Chef Maurice held up a gloved hand and started counting. "There will be Monsieur and Madame Lafoute of Chateau Lafoute. And the Lady Margaret, you remember her, the wife of Sir William's late brother? And also a Monsieur Paloni, who I am told owns a vineyard in the Napa Valley."

"Hang on, how do you know all this?"

Chef Maurice tugged down his scarf and looked over at Arthur. "I telephoned to Sir William, of course."

"Maurice, you can't just phone up your host and ask for the guest list. It's not polite!"

"But why not?" Chef Maurice looked puzzled. "One must make sure to be in good company before one accepts an invitation. It is only sensible."

"I didn't know 'sensible' was *in* your vocabulary," muttered Arthur, squinting out of the windscreen. "It's coming down fast now. I hope we'll make it back home without getting stuck. Did you say Madame Lafoute's going to be there? I thought she's almost ninety now, and apparently hates leaving Bordeaux. I wonder how Sir William managed that one."

"*Non*, it is the granddaughter, Madame Ariane Lafoute, he tells me. And her husband. He is an Englishman."

"Ah, well, at least she clearly has good taste in men. Anyone else?"

"Only a Monsieur Resnick," said Chef Maurice, watching his friend carefully.

"Charles Resnick?" yelled Arthur, gripping the steering wheel. "That blathering, cravat-wearing idiot of a wine critic? Do you know what he once said about my restaurant column?" Arthur adopted a sneering nasal tone. "'Wordington-Smythe's writing recalls to mind the Australian outback. Flat and extremely dry.'"

Chef Maurice managed to choke off a little chuckle. "There, you see, *mon ami*, if you too had telephoned to Sir William, you could have avoided this—"

"Avoid? Who said anything about avoiding? If Sir William thinks Resnick is fit to grace his table, then I'll have nothing to say about it."

"*Bon.*"

There was a moment's silence.

"And do you know another thing? When that man eats out, he goes and chooses his dishes *after* his wine, to match what he's drinking. Of all the pompous, pretentious, pontifical—"

"What do you think we will be served tonight to accompany the wines?" asked Chef Maurice, cutting Arthur off before he could run out of Resnick-suitable adjectives beginning with 'p'.

Arthur stopped mid-character-slur. "Hmm, good question. Nothing too complicated, I fancy, wouldn't want to

12

overpower the wines. If we're having whites, perhaps a savoury soufflé? Goat's cheese always goes down a treat. As for the reds, I'd plump for a roast, a leanish cut. What's your reckoning?"

Chef Maurice stared up at the roof of the car, as if in deep contemplation. "I think," he said, "we will start with a dish of poached halibut with spinach purée, served in a light bouillon infused with kaffir lime, followed by a pavé of Longhorn beef with a light Madeira sauce."

Arthur let out a groan. "Don't tell me you asked Sir William what he was serving for dinner, too?"

"Of course not." Chef Maurice looked affronted. "I telephoned to his cook, Madame Bates. It was I, in fact, who made the suggestion of the spinach purée. She was most pleased, I think, with my consultation."

"Undoubtedly so. Ah, here we are."

The tall wrought-iron gates of Bourne Hall were covered in a half-inch dusting of snow. A solitary lamp post pooled orange light onto the ground, illuminating a dark-haired man wearing a short coat and an expression of intense concentration as he paced back and forth, yelling into the phone that was clamped, or possibly frozen, to his ear.

Arthur coasted up to the gates. "I say, isn't that Chuck Paloni? As in, *the* Chuck Paloni?" He turned to Chef Maurice. "Famous actor, won a whole slew of awards, now turned Hollywood director, I hear. Not ringing any bells?"

Chef Maurice shrugged. He maintained a mild disapproval of the film industry in general, on the basis that they almost always failed to depict their characters enjoying a good meal. Or, on the rare occasions when a good meal was in progress, it would invariably be disturbed by gunfire, concealed bombs, irate spouses, or marauding aliens.

He also deplored the number of chase scenes that took place in restaurant and hotel kitchens, with completely innocent chefs being knocked aside, trays of canapés flying, as the hero runs helter-skelter from gun-wielding villains, without a thought for the catering-sized mess left in his wake. And who would be paying for all the ruined ingredients?

"I had no idea he was dabbling in vineyards now," continued Arthur. "Still, I guess these film types have to have their hobbies. He looks older than he does on screen, don't you think?"

The actor-director appeared to be in his mid-forties, his dark hair verging on salt-and-pepper, with a tall, athletic frame no doubt honed by a team of personal trainers. He glanced up at the sound of Arthur's Aston Martin approaching, shouted a hasty goodbye into his phone, and started waving frantically in their direction.

Arthur cranked down his window. "Evening. Can we offer you a lift?"

"That would be swell," said the man, climbing hastily into the back seat and huffing into his hands. "Call me Chuck, by the way," he added, in the certain knowledge that Arthur and Chef Maurice would know exactly who he was.

"Arthur Wordington-Smythe," said Arthur, offering a leather-gloved hand over his shoulder. "And this is my friend, Mr Maurice Manchot."

"Pleased to meet you, *monsieur*."

"Damn long driveway," said Paloni, staring out at the snowy landscape rolling by. "Took me almost half an hour just to get to the gate."

"And not the best weather for a stroll, either, I'm sure. They say a blizzard might be coming later."

"It better not. I've got meetings back-to-back all tomorrow. That damn big house has no cell reception, plus the main phone line's down or something, can't understand half of what that butler says sometimes. So I stepped out to make a call and the next thing I know it's like I'm trekking through Siberia. And even then there's barely a signal. Nothing like back in Napa. Back home, I can be knee-deep in my vineyards, not a building in sight, and I'm chatting to my broker in Hong Kong, crystal clear like he's standing right beside me."

"Did you fly in today?" asked Arthur.

"What? Hell no, I've been in London all week for the premiere of *The Dark Aquarium*."

"Ah, yes. That's the one with Miranda Mackenzie, am I right?" said Arthur, to show willing.

"You got it. Dynamite little actress, she is. I was the one who gave her her first big break a few years back. Dynamite, she is, in more ways than one, if you catch my drift." He aimed a big wink at Chef Maurice in the

15

rear-view mirror, possibly on the assumption that, being a Frenchman, the chef might appreciate the sentiment. Unfortunately, all he got in return was a blank stare; Chef Maurice considered today's movie starlets to be a grossly underfed and, as such, thoroughly unattractive cohort.

"So how do you know Sir William, then?" said Arthur.

"Wine," said Paloni promptly. "He was one of the first investors in the Basking Buffalo vineyards. Minority stake now, but having his name on the books sure helped a lot in those early days, I can tell you that. Gives them confidence, you know what I mean?"

"So, actor, director, now winemaker, eh?" said Arthur.

"Nah, not really. I have a guy who does all the technical stuff down at the winery. I just tell him what I like. That's the joy of having your own vineyard, you know, always having good wine to drink at the end of the day, made just to your taste."

They parked up in front of Bourne Hall, next to a rather battered Rolls-Royce and a silver Porsche with the number plate R3S NCK.

"The things that man spends his money on," muttered Arthur.

Paloni had already jumped out and was banging on the front door. A butler, wearing what Chef Maurice liked to think of as standard country-house-butler uniform—that is to say, a black tailcoat, black tie, black trousers, and shiny black shoes so clean you could eat your dinner off them—opened the door and bowed.

16

"Ah, Mr Paloni, I'm glad to see you've returned safely. We were about to send out a search—"

"No need, got a lift back with these fellas here," said Paloni, pushing past the man into the warmth of the house.

The butler turned his smooth gaze onto Chef Maurice and Arthur.

"Mr Manchot. Mr Wordington-Smythe. So good to see you back at the Hall. I trust the snow didn't give you too much trouble over the short distance?"

"No, though I'm not liking the thought of trying to get back afterwards," said Arthur, stepping inside. "And how are you, Mr Gilles?"

"Very good, sir. And it's just Gilles, sir."

"Ah, like Madonna, eh?"

Gilles gave them a brief, humourless smile, and led them through the marble-floored hallway into the handsome wood-panelled drawing room.

A young couple, presumably the Lafoutes, were seated at either end of the long divan. Lady Margaret, who they had encountered on a few previous occasions, was sat by the fire, wearing a severe grey dress that matched her hair, and pointedly ignoring all of Paloni's attempts at conversation. Paloni himself was still rubbing his hands and rotating himself slowly in front of the roaring flames, like a particularly nattily dressed kebab.

"I will inform Sir William of your arrival," said Gilles, exiting the room with another small bow.

"Arthur, how good to see you again," said an oily voice from behind them.

It was Charles Resnick, sporting a burgundy bow tie, slicked-down black hair and, thought Chef Maurice, a rather sorry excuse for a pencil moustache.

"Charles," said Arthur, with a nod. "Have you met Maurice before?"

"I don't believe so," replied Resnick, looking the chef up and down.

They shook hands. Resnick's were cold yet slightly clammy.

"So Sir William tells me you're all practically neighbours. How quaint," said Resnick. "I suppose that explains your being here. Not really your type of thing, is it, Arthur?"

Arthur coughed. "Yes, the Bourne Hall estate borders on Beakley village. Just up by Maurice's restaurant, in fact."

"Oh, your village has a restaurant?" He turned to Chef Maurice. "It must be such a drag, cooking in such a—how should we say—*pedestrian* neighbourhood."

"*Mais non*," said Chef Maurice staunchly. "My customers, they come by car from all around. In fact, we have had to make bigger the car parking, just last year."

There was a little silence.

"So, Charles, how did you come to know Sir William?" said Arthur.

"In the wine world, how does one not?" replied Resnick with a thin smile. "In fact, I now count Sir William as one of my most valued clients."

"Oh yes, I did read something about your little wine brokerage venture—"

"Coming up to twenty million turnover this year. And that's not including the auction side of the business, of course. I've been working extensively with Sir William on building up his collection in recent years. I don't know about you, but I found being *just* a critic got ever so boring."

Arthur pointedly ignored the jibe. "Surely there's a bit of a conflict of interest, no? Between your reviews and wine business?"

"Not at all," said Resnick smoothly. "My writing is purely my impartial professional opinion. And on the brokerage side, I'm merely a conduit, a facilitator of transactions. Any valuations are completely at the discretion of the client."

"I see," said Arthur. He frowned at something in the distance. "If you'll excuse me one moment, gentlemen, I see that Mr Paloni's jacket sleeve has just caught fire . . . "

Chef Maurice watched his friend hurry over to Paloni, who had also just noticed his smouldering appendage and had started leaping around like, well, a man on fire, until Arthur grabbed a nearby vase of flowers and doused him down. Lady Margaret looked up from her book, tut-tutted, then carried on reading.

"So," said Chef Maurice, searching his mind for a suitable topic of conversation. Resnick was surveying the room with a distinctly bored expression. "What do you think of this weather today?"

* * *

Flames danced on the hobs as the kitchen's back door swung open. Patrick and Alf looked up from behind a giant stockpot.

"Mind if I come in? It's brass monkeys out there."

It was PC Lucy Gavistone, the only local police officer to actually live in Beakley (and the most attractive one at that) and Patrick's not-quite-girlfriend.

They'd been on two dates so far, once to the cinema to see the latest sci-fi blockbuster (Patrick's choice) and once to a photography exhibition in Cowton entitled 'From Peaks to Valleys', which had turned out to be a collection of studies on the nude male form. (PC Lucy had spent most of that evening apologising. "I honestly thought it was going to be about Welsh landscape prints!")

Today, she was wearing a thick parka over her police uniform and a red-and-white bobble hat, which she now pulled off, shaking out her blond hair.

"Fancy a hot drink?" said Patrick, waving his ladle.

"Mmmm, mulled wine?" PC Lucy stuck her head over the pot and inhaled. "Smells gorgeous."

"It's the special Cochon Rouge recipe. Chef wanted us to make up a big batch for tomorrow, but we think he left out a few ingredients when he wrote it down. Something's not quite right."

PC Lucy dipped a teaspoon in. "Tastes good to me."

Patrick shook his head. "I'm thinking it needs a bit more orange zest. Alf, do you mind—"

"Sure, sure, I get the hint," said Alf, as he headed over to the walk-in fridge. "Give you two a moment of privacy, right? To talk?" He shot Patrick a meaningful look.

"I didn't—" began PC Lucy with a blush, as the fridge door clicked shut, but Patrick waved a hand.

"Ignore him. He's just scared of you."

"Should I be flattered?"

"Probably. Can I get you something to eat?"

"'Fraid not. I'm just going door-to-door at the moment, checking up on everyone. They say it's going to be the heaviest snowfall we've had for decades. You'd better warn your customers to hurry up. Tonight's not a night for lingering over desserts."

"We're pretty quiet at the moment," said Patrick, glancing up at the empty ticket rail. "Had a few early tables, but I think most people are staying in."

"Good." PC Lucy shook a piece of snow off her hat. "Right, I better get on. I'll try to pop back in later for a drink." She smiled up at him, and Patrick felt his insides get a little warmer, in a way that definitely had nothing to do with the mulled wine.

"Um, sounds great."

He was just being silly, he told himself. Or Alf had just been trying to wind him up. But he couldn't quite dismiss what the commis chef had said the other day, about spotting PC Lucy in Cowton last weekend, strolling around arm-in-arm with a dark-haired man who was definitely not Patrick.

Probably her brother, he'd told himself. Or maybe even her father—though PC Lucy had mentioned her family lived up in Northumbria and rarely ventured further south than York.

"You okay?" said PC Lucy, her blue eyes full of concern.

"What? Oh, yup, all good. Just thinking about the mulled wine. Actually, I wanted to ask you—"

There was a yell and a loud clatter from inside the walk-in. Alf stuck his head out. "Um, I may have put my hand a bit too close to the lobster box . . . "

PC Lucy looked at her watch. "Right, I better dash. I'll catch you later?"

Patrick nodded, torn between dealing with a possibly uncomfortable truth or a definitely uncomfortable Alf.

But PC Lucy was already halfway out the door.

Alf it was, then.

Sir William was the type of man who commanded a room's full attention. Tall and imposing, wearing an impeccably cut evening jacket, his grey beard neatly clipped, he bore down upon Chef Maurice and Arthur with his hands outstretched.

"Maurice! Arthur! Glad you made it out here. Cold as hell's doorstep out there, isn't it? Sorry to keep you waiting, just had a few matters to sort out. Have you been introduced to everyone?"

"We have not yet the pleasure, *mon ami*."

"Well, let's get started then, shall we? Now that we're all here." He strode into the middle of the room to address the young couple, who stood up as he approached them.

"Ariane, Bertie, this is Mr Maurice Manchot and Mr Arthur Wordington-Smythe, you've read his restaurant reviews in the *England Observer*, no doubt. Maurice here runs a little restaurant just down the road. Proper French fare, top-notch ingredients, and not a bad wine list too, though I must confess to having a little hand in that . . . " Sir William gave a chuckle.

Chef Maurice nodded affably. He and Sir William had their little routine, honed over the years. The latter would turn up every now and then, waxing lyrical about some hitherto unknown grape variety, or an organic producer growing vines on the slope of a volcano or suchlike, that Chef Maurice simply *had* to get onto the wine list. Chef Maurice would smile, express admiration at Sir William's superb tastes, then continue to order the same wines as he always did—though occasionally he'd slip one or two new additions onto the list just to keep Sir William happy.

"Maurice, Arthur, this is Bertie and Ariane Lafoute, of Chateau—"

"Lafoute, but of course." Chef Maurice gave a little nod. "I most enjoyed a bottle of your '82 a few years ago, but I am sad to have not had the chance to try the newer vintages."

"Not a worry, we'll be remedying that quite comprehensively this evening, I should think," said Sir William.

"There will be a few of our older vintages too," added Ariane Lafoute. She was, head to toe, best described as a classic beauty. Her dark raven hair was pulled back into a shiny chignon, and her sea-green dress draped elegantly over her slim form. A silver diamond bracelet graced one slender wrist and glittered as she held out a hand to Chef Maurice.

"*Enchantée*," she said.

"Jolly good to meet you both," said Bertie Lafoute, shaking their hands in turn. He too had the look of a classic, but the classic in this case was the weak-chinned but well-bred Englishman. He wore a grey three-piece suit and grinned the grin of a young man eager to please.

"Bertie's parents were old family friends," said Sir William, laying his hand on Bertie's narrow shoulder. "His father and I, we practically grew up together."

Bertie nodded. "My father liked to collect wines too. Nothing as serious as Uncle William's collection, of course."

"He must have been pleased then, when you married a Lafoute," said Arthur, smiling at Ariane.

Bertie's face fell momentarily. "I'm afraid both he and my mother passed away quite a few years back. But yes, I'm sure they'd have loved Ariane." He put a hand around his wife's waist, while she smiled coolly up at him.

"You took the *nom de famille* as your surname, then?" said Chef Maurice.

"Rather modern, I know," said Bertie. "But I always said

Burlington was far too near the start of the alphabet, and anyhow, it's quite nice, sharing the same name." Clearly, the option of Ariane taking her husband's name had not been on the cards. Or even in the deck.

"Margaret, do come over and say hallo," said Sir William, gesturing to his sister-in-law over by the fire.

"How lovely to see you both again," said Lady Margaret, standing up and drifting over. She turned to Sir William. "Does that mean you'll finally be joining us? You've been hidden away in your study all day, though *quite* what you do in there is a mystery to us all, I'm sure."

"Yes, Margaret, the festivities are now quite underway. I'm just finishing up the introductions. Gentlemen, you presumably already know Charles—"

"—how could we not—" muttered Arthur under his breath.

"—and finally, let me present Chuck Paloni. He's representing California tonight, and has brought along some of his vineyard's top wines, he tells me."

Paloni, who was still wringing out his sleeve over the fireplace, looked up.

"We've met. These fellas gave me a lift up your driveway. You should think about getting a cell tower out here, solve all your problems. Is the main phone line still down?"

"Gilles is looking into it," said Sir William, frowning, "though I highly doubt anyone will be coming out in this weather to fix it today."

Paloni looked glum.

At this point, Gilles glided in with a tray of fluted Champagne glasses.

"The '04 Dom Pérignon," he murmured, like a benediction.

"*Magnifique*," said Ariane, holding the glass to her nose, eyes closed.

Bertie clinked his flute against Arthur's. "Here's to tonight's tasting!"

"May the best wine win," said Resnick.

"Come now, Charles, we all know there's no such thing as 'best' when it comes to wine," said Sir William, beaming at his guests.

"Bah!" Chef Maurice lifted his glass to the light. "See, the little bubbles, the superb bouquet, the long taste—a good *Champagne* is unrivalled. No one can beat the French, *mes amis*."

"Except that they did," Arthur pointed out. He raised his glass to Paloni. "What do you say? Can California do it again tonight?"

"We'll sure try our best."

"That's the spirit!" said Sir William. He placed his glass back down on Gilles's waiting tray. "Now if you'll excuse me, I'll just pop down to the cellar to bring up the last of the wines."

"I'll come with you," said Paloni, hurrying after him. "No cheating, I promise. But I wanted to pick your brains on our latest range of Cabernet . . . "

Their voices faded as the heavy drawing room doors swung shut.

"More Champagne, sir?" said Gilles, producing a bottle from about his person.

Chef Maurice nodded in approval as the pale gold liquid swirled into his glass.

"Oh, might as well," said Arthur, proffering his own glass too. "Life's too short not to drink good wine, eh?"

There was a murmur of agreement from the other guests.

Little did they know that, for one of their party tonight, this would turn out to be altogether too true.

CHAPTER 3

Le Cochon Rouge had started out life as the old village pub, and Chef Maurice had done little to change the decor in the dining room, with its low oak beams, old stone fireplace, and fully functioning bar.

Patrick now stood behind said bar, buffing the wine glasses. At his insistence, Dorothy had already headed home in the now ankle-deep snow.

There was only one diner left, sat against the far wall across from the bar. He had only ordered one course—the confit duck with dauphinoise potatoes—and had proceeded to nurse a cup of black coffee so slowly that Patrick doubted if he would finish before the new year.

"You sure I can't call you a taxi, sir? Snow's coming down fast outside."

The stranger shook his head. He hadn't uttered a single word in the last hour.

Alf came bouncing into the dining room, a steaming mug in each hand.

"Reckon I've found the secret ingredient!"

He thumped the mugs down on the bar, spilling hot wine over the varnished surface.

"So was it the star anise in the end?" asked Patrick, taking a sniff of his mug.

"Nope. 'Twasn't the cardamom either, or the cassia bark, or the dried coconut shavings"—Alf ticked the ingredients off his wine-stained fingers—"or the horseradish, or the tarragon, or the confit garlic—"

He stopped, and looked down in puzzlement at his missing sixth finger.

"How much have you had to drink?" said Patrick.

Alf leaned over the bar and waved his mug in Patrick's face. "Don't matter, just *taste* this. Am I genius or am I genius?"

"You didn't use chef's best cognac, did you? You know how he gets about that stuff."

"Aww, come on, just give it a go."

"Fine."

As mulled wines went, it was fruity, warming, and spiced to the hilt. But there was something else in the mix, something dark and sickly, and oddly savoury . . .

"Alf," said Patrick carefully, "answer me this. Have you gone and put beef gravy in the mulled wine?"

"Just a pint." Alf grinned happily, and downed his own mug. "Good, ain't it?"

Patrick could feel his stomach disagreeing already.

"It's . . . It's . . . "—Patrick cast around for a suitable word—"*funky*. And not in a good way. And what about the vegetarians?"

Alf's shoulders slumped.

"Tell you what, let's pour this stuff down the sink, and we'll just wait until chef comes back tomorrow. Then we can make up a new batch. With the *right* ingredients."

"But chef said he'll roast my head if I don't get a batch ready for tomorrow lunch," wailed Alf. "There's that big group coming. And he was on about how we have to leave it simmering the whole night."

"Well, then, he should have written it down right in the first place," said Patrick firmly.

Alf was now clutching at his head. "Don't wanna go in the oven . . . " he muttered.

"Then you better give chef a call up at the Hall and ask him about the missing ingredient."

Alf's one remaining sober brain cell waved a little red flag. "'Tisat a good idea? Disturbing chef at his fancy dinner?"

"Well, it's your head." Patrick picked up his mug, took another sip and grimaced. And then another. It was ghastly—there was no way around that—but it was also surprisingly moreish.

He raised his mug towards the lone diner. "Want to try some of our special mulled wine, sir?" If that didn't get the man moving, he didn't know what would.

"No, thanks."

He spoke with an accent. East Coast American, was Patrick's guess.

"You sure, sir?"

The man's presence was starting to annoy him. Didn't he have a home to go to? What was he waiting for, an extremely late date? Maybe he'd been stood up and was now in denial, refusing to leave, as if that would finally confirm the night's abject failure.

The usual Cochon Rouge policy for dislodging an abandoned suitor who refused to depart (or at least stop crying into the tablecloth) was to get Chef Maurice to slt down opposite him and start commiserating in such loud tones that the luckless swain would soon flee out of sheer embarrassment.

Sadly, this wasn't an option this evening, with the restaurant empty of an audience and Chef Maurice out at dinner.

Plus, the stranger had the kind of square jaw and hint of muscled bulk under his jacket that would suggest he didn't have too many problems in the being-stood-up sphere.

"He's an *American*," hissed Alf, who was thumbing back and forth through the bookings diary in search of Sir William's phone number. "Heard him on the phone earlier."

"And?"

"Suspicious, ain't it? What's he doing here on a night like this?"

"Could be visiting the area."

"He don't look like a tourist."

Beakley was used to welcoming visitors from all around the globe, who came to the Cotswolds to coo over the little

31

thatched cottages and the gently rolling meadows. But this visitor didn't look like your typical tourist—he was dressed all in black, for one, and a large leather briefcase sat at his feet.

"Maybe he's a spy." Alf attempted a conspiratorial eyebrow raise.

"Just go make your phone call. Or I'll have to start heating up the oven."

Alf lifted the old handset to his ear and began to dial laboriously, muttering numbers under his breath.

"Hallo? Halllloooooo? Is that Bourne Hall? Halloooo?"

He dropped the phone back into its cradle.

"No answer?"

"All crackly. Like crackling." Alf giggled.

"Maybe the line's down," said Patrick, absentmindedly moving Alf's mug out of the young man's reach.

"Snowed under?" offered Alf.

Patrick noticed the lone diner was now staring at them.

"Did you just say your chef is up at Bourne Hall?" said the man.

Alf nodded. "At some fancy wine dinner."

"And the phone line's gone down?"

"Seems that way," said Patrick. "Why do you a—"

But the man was already heading out the door, pulling his phone from his pocket.

Patrick and Alf wandered over to the front window and watched the stranger as he paced up and down, punching buttons on his phone and leaving thick troughs in the snow.

"What d'you reckon that's all about? Can we lock up now?" Alf's breath huffed up the window.

"No idea. And no, we can't. He's left his briefcase here, so I guess he's coming back."

Patrick stared out of the window. The man had now stopped pacing and was talking quietly into his phone, one gloved hand shielding his mouth. The cold didn't seem to be bothering him.

"What could he possibly be up to?" He turned to his side, but Alf had disappeared. "Alf?"

"Cor, look at this!" Alf popped his head up from under one of the dining tables. "You'll never guess what he's got in here! Never seen a real one up close—"

Out of the corner of his eye, Patrick saw the man hang up and stride back towards the front door.

"Alf! Get away from there!"

"Just a sec—"

"You don't have a sec!"

There was another 'Cor!' from under the table.

The man was now just two steps from the door.

Patrick did the only thing he could think of.

He turned the lock.

Arthur and Chef Maurice settled themselves onto the long chintz settee, opposite the two Lafoutes, who had resumed their seats. Lady Margaret, after throwing the present company a disdainful look, had retired to her book and fireside roost.

Resnick was sat next to Bertie Lafoute, in a high-backed leather armchair, stroking Sir William's grey long-haired Persian cat, Waffles. It gave him the look, to Arthur's mind, of the type of gentleman who likes to plot nuclear destruction and the annihilation of superheroes in his spare time.

"You really have a way with her," said Bertie, admiring Resnick and the purring cat. "Last time I tried that, I needed four stitches on my arm. Remember, darling?"

"Yes, it was just before the harvest last year," said Ariane. "It was most inconvenient."

Bertie turned red and fell silent.

"Are you all staying here tonight?" said Arthur. "I hear Sir William did some marvellous renovation work on the guest rooms last year."

"Oh, yes, they're simply spiffing," said Bertie, regaining his enthusiasm. "We've got the east-facing suite, looking out over the lawn. It gets some brilliant morning light in the summer."

Ariane stifled a small ladylike yawn.

"So, Arthur," said Resnick, "how's the restaurant column going? I'm afraid what with all the travelling, I've not had a chance to pick up the *England Observer* in a while. Distribution's down nowadays, so I hear."

"It's down everywhere in this economy, but we're puttering along just fine, I can assure you."

"Quite. So I suppose you'll be reviewing Jean Brosse-Dent's new place? It's quite the talk of the town."

"I've got a booking next Tuesday, in fact." Arthur permitted himself a little smile. The opening of Le Faucet was the highlight of the month's culinary calendar and hotter than a Scotch bonnet sambuca. Admittedly, Arthur had had to force himself out of bed at four in the morning to make the call, and had waited an hour on hold—*England Observer* food critics were never allowed to use their own names to gain a reservation but still, it would be more than worth it.

"Lunch or dinner?"

"Dinner. They threw the diary quite wide open." In reality, they'd grudgingly offered him a ten o'clock dining slot, as if bestowing a great favour, but Resnick didn't have to know that. "Of course, it might be that they recognised my voice on the phone, but what can you do?" Arthur shrugged a world-weary shrug, as if indicating that having a voice that all top restaurant phone operators could recognise at the drop of a 'hallo' was a heavy cross he'd have to bear.

"Indeed. Well, when you go, I do recommend you try the pressed duck pâté on caramelised onion sourdough. Quite a hard one to match a wine to, but I felt I did a more than adequate job."

"Ah, you have visited already?" said Chef Maurice. He gave the now stone-faced Arthur a playful poke. "Come, *mon ami*, you must act faster."

"My dear fellow, I designed their wine menu," said Resnick. "Though I can't claim it was a hard task, not given the budget that Brosse-Dent's investors had to play with. But such an honour, to have the chance to work with such a *distinguished* chef."

It was now Chef Maurice's turn to go red in the face.

The hallway door flung open and Paloni stomped back in. He looked around at the little congregation by the fire. In this light, his grim cast of features made him look at least a decade older.

"Save me some fizz, will ya? I need to go make a business call."

The door slammed shut, and they could hear him marching up the big oak staircase in the hallway.

"I thought the telephone did not work," said Chef Maurice.

"From the look on his face, I think that was a euphemism for 'I really need to go thump something'," whispered Arthur.

"Ah, I see."

"Wonder what got into *his* bonnet," said Resnick.

Waffles, who until this point had been accepting Resnick's attentions like a quietly regal pile of fur, gave a sudden yowl, leapt off the wine critic's lap and disappeared into the dining room.

"Gosh, what's got into her?" said Bertie.

"You can never tell with cats," said Arthur, a dog person through and through. "Can't tell what they're thinking, never know what they're up to when you're not looking."

"They say cats can see things that people cannot," said Ariane, her gaze darting to the dark corners of the room.

36

"It seems, Monsieur Resnick, that the cat has marked you as her territory," said Chef Maurice.

Resnick looked down. His trousers and jacket were now covered in long grey cat hairs.

"I think," he said, standing up with an obvious conscious effort not to shake himself down, "I will retire upstairs to change for dinner."

He stalked off, but not before shooting a venomous stare towards the dining room.

This left the four of them, not counting Lady Margaret, who had dozed off by the fire.

"Did you travel from Bordeaux this morning?" asked Chef Maurice.

"Oh no, we were in London before this," said Bertie. "Seeing old friends, meeting a few potential investors. Chuck gave us a lift down this morning, or at least his driver did. Quite a bit of luck, he's staying at the same place as us near Piccadilly."

"The Belvedere," said Ariane. "We always stay there when we are in London."

"They have simply the best beds in town," enthused Bertie. "I don't know how they do it. I'm a terrible sleeper back home, tossing and turning all night, but give me a bed at The Belvedere and I'm out like a lamb."

"Impressive," said Arthur, who personally rated hotels based on the availability and quality of the complimentary slippers. "So I take it you're already acquainted with our famous filmmaker then?"

"A little," said Ariane, with a shrug. "He came to Chateau Lafoute a few years ago to see our vineyard processes. He said he wished to bring out the flavours of Bordeaux from the *terroir* of the Napa Valley," she added with a mildly amused expression.

"Come on, darling, one has to admit he's made a rather good job of it so far, you even said it yourself."

"Thanks more to the winemaker he pays, I am sure." Ariane looked up at the clock on the mantelpiece. "Do excuse me, *chéri*, but I think if Sir William is not starting the dinner yet, I will go close my eyes for a short moment. I have a headache beginning."

She stood up, the light from the fire flickering off her silken dress.

"So you've known Sir William a long time then," said Arthur to Bertie.

"What? Oh, yes, for yonks," said Bertie, watching his wife sashay out of the room. "Used to come here all the time as a boy. Spent my summers here too when I was up at Oxford." He rubbed his eyes. "Makes you wonder where the years go . . . "

"Come on, now you're talking like us oldies," said Arthur, while Chef Maurice gave a short harrumph to indicate he did not consider himself one of their number either. "What are you, barely thirty, I'd bet?"

"Just turned thirty, actually."

"There you go. And running one of the finest vineyards in the world. Not a bad show."

"Well, they're not exactly mine," said Bertie, though he managed a wistful smile. He glanced towards the door. "If you'll excuse me a moment, I'll just go and make sure Ariane is feeling okay."

"Is it us? Did I forget to wear cologne?" said Arthur, as he and Chef Maurice sat there holding their Champagne glasses, the room now empty save for the genteel snores coming from Lady Margaret's chair.

Chef Maurice, who usually slapped on the cologne like it was water, clicked his tongue.

"*Mon ami*, do not tell me you are wearing cologne? For a wine tasting, one's senses must be sharp and the air pure, free from scents and *les parfums*."

"Who's the sudden wine buff now?" said Arthur, gazing towards the dining room door, which was ajar from when Waffles had made her escape. "Come on, let's go see how Gilles is getting on. We might even get a sneak peek of the wines for tonight."

In the dining room—a long, handsome room dominated by a glittering chandelier overhead—they found Gilles not, as expected, buffing the cutlery for the tenth time, but instead staring out of one of the tall windows that gave onto the Bourne Hall lawns, now iced with a thick layer of snowfall.

He started as they entered, then smoothly drew the curtains.

"How's the snow looking?" said Arthur.

"At least a foot deep now, sir," said Gilles, moving over to the table to straighten an errant fish knife. Arthur made

39

an attempt to tally up the wine glasses on the table, but happily gave up after losing count twice.

"The lake will most certainly be frozen over. Do either of you gentlemen skate?"

"Not since I was a little boy. Nowadays, though, the thought of falling over, and those flashing blades . . . " Arthur gave a little shudder.

"I, myself, am an excellent skater," said Chef Maurice.

"You are?" Arthur looked his friend up and down. If you were the kind of person to describe body shapes via the medium of vegetables, Chef Maurice would most likely be an extra-large turnip. It was hard to imagine him doing anything as aerodynamic as ice-skating. Though, perhaps, he could be useful as an early warning system for detecting patches of thin ice . . .

"You have not seen me do the skating?" said Chef Maurice with surprise. "Perhaps then we will ask Sir William if he will allow us onto his lake later this week."

Gilles, having probably shared the same vision as Arthur, looked visibly alarmed. "I hear that this cold weather is unlikely to last long. In which case I am not sure if the lake will freeze to a sufficient extent for skating. Perhaps for safety's sake, it would be better to wait for a more opportune climate."

Like the next ice age, thought Arthur.

"Have you been with Sir William a long time, Gilles?" he asked.

"Fifteen years this January, sir."

"Golly, that long, eh? Still enjoying it? The butlering?"

"Very much so, sir," said Gilles, pulling one of the chairs a millimetre further out from the tablecloth. Down the centre of the table was a long row of wine bottles, each covered with a smart black cotton bag with a numeral sewn on. A few places were empty, presumably ready for the bottles Sir William had gone to fetch.

"We've been especially busy this year with the expansion of the wine cellar, which brings the whole collection together in one place for the first time. Sir William has also had me assisting him with the update of the cataloguing system."

"Ah, a database and whatnot?"

Gilles wrinkled his nose. "I'm afraid we're not quite that modern, sir. It's a simple cellar book. Name, producer, vintage, source, date acquired, that kind of thing." He noticed Arthur's expression. "It's a significant improvement on what we had before, I assure you."

"Ah, and what was that?" said Chef Maurice.

Gilles smiled faintly. "Scraps of paper, the odd receipt. One does marvel at the miraculous filing properties of an old shoebox."

"Indeed. So any chance of a hint about tonight's wi—"

Arthur stopped, as a huffing sound from the drawing room grew louder and a middle-aged woman in a blue gingham apron burst in. If Chef Maurice was turnip-shaped, then she was possibly a medium-sized radish. Her face, at least, was currently the right colour.

"Gilles . . . the cellar . . . Sir William . . ."

41

"Breathe, Mrs Bates, breathe," said Gilles, quickly sitting the panting cook down into a nearby chair. "Now tell me, what has happened?"

She stared up into his concerned face.

"He won't unlock the cellar door! Oh, Gilles, I think something terrible's happened to Sir William!"

CHAPTER 4

The residents of Beakley were all tucked up warm in their cottages, though some of the older kids had taken the opportunity to start building snowmen and other icy sculptures on the village green.

PC Lucy was particularly impressed with the life-sized Vauxhall Astra, which she'd tried to take down the number plate of—it was illegally parked in the middle of the green, after all—until she realised it was entirely made of snow.

She hoped no one had seen her. The local kids would never let her live *that* one down.

Policing duty done, she was looking forward to a nice glass of mulled wine in front of Le Cochon Rouge's big stone fireplace.

And seeing Patrick, of course. But currently, with her fingers numb and her toes having cut off communications several hours ago, she was mostly looking forward to the fire.

She knocked on Le Cochon Rouge's back door and stepped inside to be met with a rather odd scene.

Alf was crouched under the main kitchen workbench, clutching a tea towel, while Patrick paced back and forth. He always looked so good, thought PC Lucy, when he had that darkly serious, knitted-brow look going on . . .

"Is something wrong?"

Alf pointed an unsteady finger towards the dining room. "He's got a gun. A gun! You gotta go save chef!"

PC Lucy peered under the table for a moment into Alf's unfocused eyes, then looked up at Patrick.

"Has he been drinking?"

"All night. He's been testing the mulled wine recipes."

"Ah, well that explains that. He's drunk as a skunk. What's this about a gun?"

Alf clutched at her leg. "He's gonna shoot chef!"

PC Lucy looked at Patrick again. "Is he?"

"I don't know, I didn't see any gun. Alf went looking through one of the customers' briefcase when he went outside to take a call. Yes, I know," he added, seeing her appalled expression, "but anyway, I stalled the guy at the door and got Alf back here to the kitchen."

"And what's all this about shooting Maurice? I know he rubs people up the wrong way sometimes, but it's a bit of an overreaction, no matter what he's done this time."

"I don't think he's done anything," said Patrick, rubbing his forehead. "And the guy did seem weirdly interested when we tried to give chef a call up at Bourne Hall."

"He wanted to talk to him?"

"I don't know, the line was down. We told him that, and he dashed out to make a call."

"Hmm. Odd."

PC Lucy stuck her head into the main dining room to get a look at the lone visitor. If he was going for the hired-killer look he was doing a good job of it, she thought. Black jacket, black polo neck, black jeans, black boots. Close-cropped white-blond hair. He was staring intently at his watch, as if waiting for it to explode.

He looked up at her, and she ducked back into the kitchens.

"Well, he's not doing anything particularly suspicious. Apart from sitting in a restaurant on the coldest night of the year with a snowstorm blowing outside. Is he stuck here?"

Patrick shook his head. "He kept refusing to let me call him a taxi. Can you at least, uh, go out and search his briefcase?"

"Patrick, I can't just randomly search members of the public for no good reason. Not without 'reasonable grounds', and I'm afraid Alf really doesn't qualify at this point."

Alf tugged on her trouser leg. "But what about chef?"

PC Lucy sighed. "Okay, I'll go have a word with your mysterious stranger, find out what he's waiting for, make sure he's got a home to go to. Maybe he's been stood up for a date or something."

Unlikely, she added to herself. Who'd stand up a man with a jawline like that?

She shrugged out of her parka and pulled off the bobble hat—not a good look when aiming to command authority—and headed into the dining room.

It was empty.

"He's gone," she said, returning to the kitchens.

"What?" said Patrick and Alf in unison.

Rather than relief, both their faces registered sudden alarm.

Alf scrambled out from under the table. "He's gone after chef!"

"Do you *really* think he's gone to look for Maurice?" said PC Lucy to Patrick.

"I got the impression he was more interested in Bourne Hall. Like he was trying to get hold of someone there and couldn't."

Alf had run out into the backyard and was pointing into the distance. PC Lucy and Patrick followed him, trudging through the knee-deep snow. In the field behind the restaurant, picked out by the faint moonlight, was a tall dark figure trekking steadily across the whiteness.

"We've gotta follow him! That's the way to Bourne Hall!"

PC Lucy and Patrick shared a look, then grabbed Alf by the shoulders and dragged him back inside.

"You've gotta believe me. I'm not stupid, I know a gun when I see one!"

PC Lucy looked over Alf's head at Patrick. "So what do we do now?"

"Well, if we set off right this minute, he won't be hard to follow, what with the tracks in the snow—"

"I *meant* about Alf."

But Patrick was already pulling on his coat and gloves.

"Wait, you're not seriously going after that guy, are you?"

"He's up to something, I'm sure of it. And why not?"

He's got a gun, thought PC Lucy, then shook herself. People didn't just carry guns around, not here in England. There had to be another explanation. Plus the police made sure people didn't just go around carrying illegal weapons.

She looked down at her badge.

Dammit.

"Fine. But we're not approaching him, okay? We'll just see where he's going."

They left Alf wrapped in a blanket in the corner of the kitchen, with strict instructions to lock the door behind them.

"One moment." Patrick stopped, strode over to the hob, grabbed a large stockpot and poured the contents down the sink.

"Oooooaawwww," said Alf, at the sound of his night's work sloshing down the plughole.

"Right, now we can go."

The Bourne Hall wine cellar door was located behind the main staircase in the hallway. It was seven feet tall, made of solid oak and carved with a tasteful border of grapes and vines.

47

"I was just getting the canapés ready and thought I'd ask Sir William if he wanted the little Yorkshire puds first or last, you know how they're his favourite, so I came out"—Mrs Bates waved at the kitchen door, which faced the cellar from across the corridor—"to check with him, but the cellar door was all closed and wouldn't budge. I knocked and knocked, but the master, he ain't answering!"

Gilles tried the doorknob.

"Locked," he said gravely. He gave a loud rap on the door. "Sir? Sir William? Is there a problem?"

"'Course there's a problem," sobbed Mrs Bates. "It's not like him not to answer, especially not with guests and everyone waiting for him."

She hammered on the door with her fists.

"Does he usually lock the door when he's down there?" said Arthur.

The butler shook his head. "Not normally. Only when he doesn't want to be disturbed."

Chef Maurice bent down and put his eye to the keyhole. It was all black. He gave the keyhole a good sniff too.

"In the case of poisonous gas," he explained as he caught Arthur's look.

There was the clatter of footsteps on the stairs.

"What's going on?" It was Bertie, looking puzzled, closely followed by Paloni, straightening his bow tie.

"The master's gone and locked himself in the cellar and ain't answering!"

"Maybe the door's jammed with all this cold weather," said Paloni. "Happened to me once in Vermont, at this—"

"Then why's he not answering?" Mrs Bates pounded on the door again. "Sir William, if you can hear me, you open up this door right this minute!"

"What is happening?" Ariane floated down the stairs. Her eyes were slightly red from sleep. "Who is in there?"

"We think Sir William might have had an accident," said Arthur. "He's locked the door, and isn't answering."

"Well, isn't there a second key?" said Resnick, who'd caught the end of the conversation as he hurried down behind Ariane, his bow tie hanging around his neck and his jacket undone.

"I believe there is a spare key in the safe in Sir William's study. I will see if I can procure it," said Gilles, disappearing back down the corridor.

"You!" said Bertie, advancing on Paloni, who gave him the look a bull would give a particularly uppity sheep. "You were down there with him a moment ago. What happened?"

"What? Nothing!"

"What do you mean, nothing? You mean he was completely fine when you left him?"

"Of course he was!"

"Are you sure? And what did you need to speak to him so badly about in the first place?"

Paloni hesitated. "Just winery business," he said finally. "Wanted his advice. No, thanks," he added, as Chef

Maurice proffered the tray of goat's cheese and red onion tartlets that he'd found going cold in the kitchen.

"Who's making that infernal racket?" said Lady Margaret, coming out of the drawing room, book in hand.

"The master's gone and locked himself in the cellar, ma'am," said Mrs Bates.

"Can't say I blame him. I told him throwing all these parties would wear him out eventually. A nice quiet evening with a book, that's what you need, I told him."

Gilles returned, walking fast and carrying a key-shaped lump of red wax.

"Sir William gave you the code to his safe, but keeps the spare cellar key in wax? How oddly . . . untrusting," said Resnick with a sneer.

Gilles broke the wax open and turned the key in the door. There was a click and a whirring sound, and the door swung backwards. It was now evident that the carved oak was merely a facade, hiding a thick steel door lined with deadbolts all around.

"Gosh, when did that happen?" said Bertie. "It wasn't like that last June."

"Sir William had new security measures installed over the summer. I advised him on the design, after he made some rather valuable additions to the collection," said Resnick.

They descended the stairs, Gilles leading the way, closely followed by Bertie. Chef Maurice brought up the rear, supporting a weak-kneed Mrs Bates.

"Sir William, are you there—" Gilles voice strangled to a stop, mid-sentence.

Chef Maurice, dragging the poor Mrs Bates, hurried down the last steps. They rounded the corner of the stairwell to find the others frozen in place, staring at the scene before them.

Sir William was laid out on the floor, motionless, a broken wine bottle beside him and a terrible gash on his neck.

"Is he . . . ?" breathed Ariane.

Gilles, his face drained of colour, knelt down carefully beside his master and applied two fingers to the man's wrist.

He nodded. "He's dead."

CHAPTER 5

Patrick pulled his hat further down over his ears, stuffed his gloved hands deeper into his pockets, and tried not to think about snow, ice, icicles, ice cubes, ice cream, and other chilly topics.

In the moonlight, the stranger's footprints were dark pits in the snow, leading endlessly over the fields behind the restaurant.

"Why couldn't he have taken the main road?" said Patrick, his breath misting the air.

"If he's heading to Bourne Hall, then this is the quickest way," said PC Lucy. "The gate on the main road is nowhere near the house itself."

"So he knows the layout of Bourne Hall, then."

"Looks like it."

The black-clad man was nowhere in sight. Patrick liked to think of himself as a fairly fit specimen—it was amazing what lugging copper pots all day would do for your biceps—but it was dawning on him that chefs were built for power over short distances, such as between the walk-in and hobs.

Plus, professional kitchens never got this *cold*.

At least the snow had now stopped falling, leaving the air icy fresh. The low hills around Beakley were soft and pristine in the moon's glow. It was almost romantic, if you ignored the fact they were on the trail of a potential gun-toting killer.

Perhaps now was a good time to tackle the matter of the *other* mystery man . . .

"So, um, did you get up to much last weekend? Sorry I had to work."

"What?" PC Lucy was a good head shorter than Patrick, and keeping up the pace was clearly exerting her. But it was equally clear that if he slowed down, she'd take it as a deadly insult and probably never speak to him again. "Oh, no, not much. I was on shift all of Saturday, so I had a lazy Sunday. TV, pyjamas, didn't see a soul. Blissful, really."

"So you didn't go out at all?"

"No. Why, something wrong with that?"

"No! I just thought, um, you might have been seeing family, or something."

"Family? You've got to be kidding. You'd need a crowbar to get my parents further than five miles from their farm. Plus I'll soon be up there for Christmas."

"What about your, uh, brother?" It was a stab in the dark, Patrick knew, but he refused to stew any longer over what might be a simple misunderstanding.

PC Lucy gave him a strange look. "I don't have a brother. Only child, remember?"

Patrick didn't remember, but he knew better than to admit to the crime of not having listened fully at some point on their last two dates.

"So, Mr Nosy Parker, what did *you* get up to at the weekend?"

"Me? Well, we had a few early Christmas parties at the restaurant, so we were pretty busy. Plus Alf was off all Sunday. I think he went into Cowton to do his Christmas shopping."

He watched her face carefully for any admission of guilt, but got no reaction.

"Didn't think Alf was that organised. Just goes to show, eh?"

She halted suddenly, and pointed to a deep rectangular depression in the snow.

The stranger had stopped here to take something out of his briefcase.

Patrick's heart started beating louder.

"Maybe he just got cold and wanted a hat and scarf," said PC Lucy.

Even so, they both picked up the pace.

PC Lucy felt bad. Not from the snow slowly dripping into her faux-fur-lined boots, nor the biting wind that was threatening to freeze her nose off. But from the fact that she'd just lied.

She'd lied to Patrick.

And she *liked* Patrick. She really did. He was smart, and funny, and good-looking in that dark, wavy-haired Clark

Kent way, minus the occasional urge to run around in tights and red underpants (as far as she knew).

But that was it. She didn't know him that well, yet. Soon, she promised herself, she'd tell him the truth.

But not just yet.

They walked on in silence through the crunching snow.

After a quick search of the cellar, in case the attacker was still present, Gilles ushered the stunned guests up the stairs, then carefully locked the cellar door and pocketed the key.

Following some unspoken search for comfort—or perhaps because Chef Maurice had been first up the stairs and naturally gravitated towards food preparation areas—they found themselves huddled in the Bourne Hall kitchens.

"If the ladies and gentlemen will remain here," said Gilles, "I will conduct a quick search of the building, in case the . . . perpetrator is hiding somewhere still."

Mrs Bates gave a little wail from her rocking chair by the stove. Bertie was sat at the table with his arm around Ariane, talking quietly in soothing tones.

"I'll come with you," said Paloni, glancing around and snatching up a heavy-based saucepan to accompany them.

"I suppose we'd better call the police," said Resnick. "Though in these parts, who knows how long they'll take to turn up."

Arthur, who found himself nearest to the wall-hung phone, picked up the receiver and held it to his ear.

"Line's still down," he reported. "Nothing but crackle."

"Surely that can't be a coincidence," said Bertie, looking pale.

"Really?" said Resnick. "I understood the line had been down since this afternoon. Surely someone would have noticed an intruder sneaking around all that time."

"Not necessarily," said Lady Margaret, crisply. "It's a big house. My Timothy used to hide for hours in all the nooks and crannies, and only a good gingerbread cake would get him to come out. Plenty of places to hide in here."

With that, she flipped open her book and started reading.

There was a series of clinks and clatters as Chef Maurice conducted a thorough investigation of the cupboards in search of a coffee pot.

"There's loose tea and some instant coffee in the drawer over there," said Mrs Bates, who'd perked up at the sound of another cook invading her professional space.

"Pah, instant coffee," muttered Chef Maurice, and continued on until he unearthed a slightly tarnished coffee pot and an unopened bag of fresh grounds.

"How many?" he said.

All hands shot up, except for Mrs Bates, who deplored such a patently European habit and went to fill up the teapot.

The coffee had barely brewed when Gilles and Paloni returned, their faces grim. Mrs Bates bustled over and grabbed the saucepan out of Paloni's hands.

"My best pan, that is," she tutted.

"We found where he got in," said Paloni. "Broken window in the storeroom right next to here. Glass all over the shop."

"The intruder must have waited to enter the cellar after Mr Paloni left Sir William," said Gilles. "Presumably it was he who locked the cellar door after."

"But why would he do that?" said Ariane. Her eyes were wide, and she was clutching Bertie's arm.

"To slow us down and distract us, clearly," said Resnick. "Give him time to make his escape."

"A plausible explanation, sir," said Gilles. "Has anyone telephoned the police?"

They explained the crackly phone line.

"Very well. If you will excuse me, I will walk down to the main road. There is a telephone box not far from the gates. The police must be notified immediately."

"I'll go too," said Bertie, though there was a slight tremor in his voice.

"So will I," said Resnick.

"And me," said Paloni.

Arthur looked around and realised he'd have to volunteer too, for the look of the thing. Thankfully, Gilles spoke first.

"If you will allow me, gentlemen, I do not think it needs so many of us. Mr Lafoute and I will go to telephone the police. Perhaps the rest of you gentlemen could stay here and look after the ladies."

Lady Margaret looked up from her book with an unimpressed stare. "I think you will find we are quite capable of looking after ourselves."

"Of course, ma'am," said Gilles with a bow, then beat a hasty retreat with Bertie on his tail.

Paloni lost no time in settling himself next to Ariane, draping his dinner jacket over her bare shoulders, and was soon engaged in a low, murmuring conversation.

Mrs Bates gave a sudden cry and hurried over to the warming oven. She extracted a large tray of mini Yorkshire puddings, complete with mini sausages and dollops of thick gravy.

"They were his favourite," she said quietly.

The assembled guests had, however, lost their appetites. Arthur managed two, while Chef Maurice stepped in to polish off the lot—no doubt for Mrs Bates' sake.

"Madame Bates, when was the last time that you saw Sir William?" asked Chef Maurice, sitting down with his second cup of coffee.

"It was just when he was going down to the cellar with Mr Paloni," said Mrs Bates. "He popped his head in here and asked me to get the canapés ready to go."

"And when was this?"

Mrs Bates looked up at the clock over the sink.

"Was just a few minutes after seven," she said. "I remember because the tartlets take ten minutes to warm through, and I was going to get the first trays ready for quarter past."

"And the door to the kitchen, it was open all the time?"

Mrs Bates nodded. "But I was racing all over the place, single-minded I am. I don't think I'd have noticed any-

58

thing happening out there." Her hands trembled. "Do you think I might have seen—"

"Ah, you must not worry yourself about that. A criminal makes sure to not be seen. But do you remember seeing Monsieur Paloni leaving the cellar?"

"That I did. Came storming out, he did. I remember laughing to myself because he tried to slam the door"—she shot a quick look over to Paloni, but he was still occupied with Ariane—"except it ain't that kind of door and swings ever so slow."

Chef Maurice lowered his voice. "And you did not see him lock it?"

Mrs Bates shook her head. "He was gone before it even closed. Plus, I'd have remembered something like that. Only the master or Gilles ever has a key. He just walked off, he did."

Arthur looked up at the clock. "It was around half past when Mrs Bates came to get us in the dining room. So that gives the intruder about fifteen minutes to get in, get down to the cellar, and get out. Tight, but more than possible."

"I told William he should get better locks on all the windows," said Lady Margaret severely. "These roving madmen, they'll be the death of us all."

This set Mrs Bates off into another chorus of sobs.

"Now, now," said Arthur, reaching out to pat the cook, his hand hovering uncertainly before settling for an outer-lying expanse of elbow. "Whoever it was, he won't be coming back. No one would take that risk."

"You are sure it was a madman, *mon ami*?" said Chef Maurice.

"Of course!"

The other guests nodded. Of course it had to have been.

Because if it wasn't a madman, so their collective thoughts ran, it must have been one of them.

CHAPTER 6

Patrick struggled to the top of the hill, PC Lucy trudging along in his wake. From here, he could see the little squares of light that picked out the eastern side of Bourne Hall. They must have still been half a mile away, but from this vantage point, he could see the dark footprints stretching down the slope before them.

And, in the distance, the blond-haired, black-clad stranger.

"We'd better hurry up. He's almost at the Hall," said PC Lucy, reaching his side. She grabbed his hand and they ran skidding down the slope.

Reaching the flat fields below, they pounded through the thick snow, which slowed their steps and pushed back at them like an invisible hand. Thankfully, their quarry didn't seem to have noticed them closing the distance on him.

They might have made it, too, if a hidden tree root hadn't snagged Patrick around the ankle and sent him flying across the ground.

A few frosty moments later, he raised his head out of his self-created snow drift. They were less than twenty metres from the Hall, and the man had almost reached the nearest side door.

"Please tell me Sir William at least locks his doors at night," PC Lucy muttered, as she slid an arm under Patrick to try and lift him up. "I hand out leaflets every year, and every year I can stroll into most of the village's—"

There was a burst of warm light as the door flung open, and the man disappeared inside.

There comes a point in a man's life when he must boldly go, and this point had come on, rather suddenly, for Arthur. So, recruiting Chef Maurice as backup, and instructing Paloni to send out a search party in the event of their non-return, they set out for the east wing of Bourne Hall in a quest to visit the bathroom facilities.

Chef Maurice had borrowed another of Mrs Bates' frying pans, on the promise that he would avoid attacking any intruders with the side with the non-stick coating.

To get to the east wing, they had to pass through the drawing room again, which was now shrouded in an eerie silence. Empty glasses littered the coffee table, and the fire had burned low in the grate, casting long shadows over the carpet.

Chef Maurice stuck his head into the dining room. The masked bottles, corks untouched, stood there patiently—judgement would have to wait another day.

The bathroom was located down a cold corridor off the main drawing room. The walls were lined with faded fleur-de-lis wallpaper, and a long display cabinet stood to one side, filled with ranks of polished silverware.

"Only be a moment," said Arthur, ducking into the bathroom. "Keep an eye out for anything suspicious," he added, his voice muffled by the thick door.

Chef Maurice wandered over to the silverware display, and inspected his moustache with the aid of a large silver tea tray.

"I say, this is an original Crapper!" came Arthur's voice through the bathroom door. "Thomas Crapper & Co., Sanitary Engineers, it says here. Fine old firm. They say his father . . ."

Chef Maurice tuned out from Arthur's ablutionary rhapsodies and concentrated on his own bladder control. Of course, any chef who'd spent time in a busy kitchen developed an iron bladder, but the evening's turn of events had apparently unsettled even his own normally stout constitution.

A flicker in the silverware and a creak of a floorboard drew his attention to the end of the corridor. A tall man, dressed head to toe in black, emerged from a side door. There was snow on his hat and boots, and he was carrying a leather briefcase. He started at the sight of Chef Maurice, then reached into his jacket.

"I'm—" he began, but stopped.

This was because Chef Maurice had raised his trusty frying pan above his head and was pounding towards the intruder, bellowing like a berserker warrior.

Kitchens are generally noisy environments, and Chef Maurice could bellow with the best of them.

"Aaaaaaaaaeeeeeeeeeeiiiiiiiiiiiiiiii!"

The man gave him one look, and turned and ran.

Arthur was just drying his hands when he heard the demonic yell from outside.

"All right, all right, I'm almost done. No need to yell like that," he called.

He drew the lock and pulled open the door.

The corridor was empty, save for a small patch of melting snow down the other end. A frosty breeze was sneaking its way into the building through the open doorway.

"Argh!" came a cry from somewhere outside, and the sound of scuffling.

It had been a male voice, but definitely not Chef Maurice.

Picking up a nearby candlestick, Arthur edged his way over to the door.

Patrick lay in the snow, trying to piece together the last forty seconds.

They had almost reached Bourne Hall when the same side door had been flung back and the blond-haired man had come sprinting out, crashing straight into Patrick.

The man had landed right on top of him, his briefcase dealing Patrick a nasty jab to the kneecap. Then his attacker had scrambled to his feet and taken off back across the fields.

Completely winded, he'd rolled over to see PC Lucy— who'd been some ten metres behind—running towards him.

"Patrick, are you—"

A bellowing sound erupted from the open doorway.

"Aaaaaeeeeeeeeeeeeeeeiiiiiiiiiiii— *Eh?*"

The frying pan halted its descent a few inches above Patrick's nose, and was quickly replaced by the only mildly less alarming sight of Chef Maurice bending over him.

"Patrick? What do you do out here in the snow? It is not the time for making the snow angels. We are under attack!"

"Wha— Why—"

"What the hell was all that?" PC Lucy rushed over to Patrick and knelt down. "Are you okay?"

"Just winded. Nothing broken. I think." He tested his knee gingerly.

"Ah, Mademoiselle Lucy, you have arrived. That was very fast, most impressive."

"What?"

"You received our call, did you not?" He looked at her blank face. "They did not tell you what has happened? That is bad communication! For the prevention of crime, information must flow like hot oil. It is imperative—"

"Maurice! What on earth are you on about?"

He paused, finger raised in mid-lecture.

"Sir William, he has been murdered. That is why you are here, *non?* But why do you bring Patrick?"

PC Lucy gaped at him.

Chef Maurice looked down in puzzlement at his sous-chef, then light dawned in his eyes.

"Ah, I forget! You must also add the brandy-soaked nutmegs. They are in the fridge."

"Whuh . . . " said Patrick, still a little behind events.

"For the mulled wine. This is why you also come, is it not?"

"I think," said PC Lucy, hauling Patrick to his feet, "we better go inside and find out what the heck is going on."

CHAPTER 7

If Gilles or Bertie were surprised to find a police officer already at the Hall when they returned from their trek, they were too polite to make any comment.

Gilles thanked PC Lucy for her prompt arrival, while Bertie made a beeline for the kitchen's wood-burning stove.

The cellar key was produced and Gilles led PC Lucy down the stone steps. They were followed by Chef Maurice, still *avec* trusty frying pan, ready to protect PC Lucy should any more intruders be found; Arthur, ready to protect Chef Maurice should PC Lucy lose her temper and attempt to strangle him; and lastly Patrick, who felt, as PC Lucy's not-quite-boyfriend, he should not be seen to be upstaged by his boss in this protection racket.

PC Lucy crouched down next to the body, trying to maintain a mask of professional blankness while her insides did somersaults.

"What do you think happened?" said Patrick, next to her.

PC Lucy leaned closer to the body, careful not to disturb anything.

"We'll have to wait for the forensics report to be certain, but it looks like he was hit on the back of the head with something heavy, probably a wine bottle, given these cuts. Then they went for the throat . . . " She glanced down at the dark pool which had spread across the flagstones.

"With that, you think?" Patrick pointed at the remains of a wine bottle, the cork and neck still intact, but the body smashed in to leave a jagged, razor-sharp edge.

PC Lucy nodded.

"Any chance of fingerprints?"

"I doubt it." She had noticed a soft, slightly grubby cloth lying nearby, presumably used by Sir William or Gilles to wipe dust from the bottles. It was now splattered with bloodstains. "But we'll send it off to the lab anyhow. You never know."

Chef Maurice, bending over the body, shuffled around to PC Lucy's side.

"His arm like that, perhaps this has some meaning?"

Sir William's left arm lay flung out to one side, his head tilted in the same direction.

They all looked up at the display cabinet opposite, which housed a collection of very large old bottles of wine in a temperature-controlled environment. There were roughly thirty in total, with a few of the stands still empty.

"Why are they so big?" asked PC Lucy.

"They're magnums," said Patrick. "Double the size of a normal bottle, so one and a half litres each."

"Magnum?" said PC Lucy. "Like the gun? And the ice cream?"

"That's right. Though I'm not sure there's much of a connection there . . . "

"Funny, I've never seen them in a restaurant," said PC Lucy, still staring at the cabinet. "Are they common?"

"*Non*, it is usual for only the chateaux with great prestige to produce magnums and bigger," said Chef Maurice. "Especially for the old vintages like the ones here. The making of magnums, it is expensive, you see."

PC Lucy ran her gaze along the display cabinet once more, then shook her head. If Sir William had been shot, or possibly stabbed with an ice cream stick, the collection of magnums might just have been a clue. As such, she moved on with her search.

She slid a careful hand into Sir William's dinner jacket pocket but, as she expected, there was nothing there. Sir William didn't seem the kind of man who would ruin the line of his tailoring by carrying around unnecessary items, especially not in his own home.

However, the other pocket revealed a folded piece of lilac notepaper.

Darling, wait up for me tonight, I will slip out as soon as I can. I cannot wait to have you. A.

The handwriting was curly, expansive, passionate, even. A woman's handwriting.

Chef Maurice, reading over her shoulder, clicked his tongue. "*Oh là là*, the poor Monsieur Bertie."

"A is for . . . ?" PC Lucy had been hurriedly introduced to the guests upstairs, but hadn't had time to take down names.

"Ariane Lafoute," said Arthur. He was standing in a corner as far away as possible, staring at a wall stacked with wine crates. Dead bodies were not his forte, as he had discovered only a few months previously. "Married to Bertie, the young chap who came in with Gilles. But, well, it's a bit hard to believe, isn't it? I mean, Sir William is, was, hardly the type of fellow to fool around with another man's wife. And Bertie's practically family to him. You saw the way he talked."

"But there are no other A's present here in the house. Except for you, *mon ami*," pointed out Chef Maurice.

Three faces turned to Arthur, who spluttered:

"Well, *I* certainly didn't write that note. If you ask me, it looks a lot like Maurice's handwriting. Very French, I can see even from here."

"Bah! I object! How could I—"

"Okay, gentlemen, enough," said PC Lucy, holding up a hand. "And it goes without saying, you are *not* to mention this note to anyone, understand?"

There were vigorous nods all around, which meant, she knew from experience, exactly nothing.

She placed the lilac-coloured note in a plastic bag for safekeeping, and reached gingerly into Sir William's nearest trouser pocket. Her fingers closed around something heavy and metallic.

It was a large brass key, hung on a thick woven cord.

She looked over at Chef Maurice.

"I thought you said the intruder locked the door behind him. Or her," she added. Crime, after all, was an equal opportunities employer. "From the *outside*."

"But it is true! It was most definitely locked when Madame Bates came for us. Unless . . . *Un moment*. Let us not jump on conclusions." Chef Maurice grabbed the key and hurried up the stairs. A moment later, there was a whirring noise and a click.

"*Oui*, this is the correct key," he said, as he returned down the stairs.

"Then how . . . ?" PC Lucy looked around the room. The cellar was big by normal standards, but bottles and small wine crates lined every available wall. There was nowhere for anyone to hide. "What about a second key?"

Chef Maurice shook his head. "It was in wax. We saw Monsieur Gilles break it open before us. It could not have been used before."

PC Lucy checked the other trouser pocket, but found only a clean white handkerchief. She pushed it back in.

"Right, let's get back upstairs," she said.

Chef Maurice remained squatted down for a moment, then reached out and laid a gentle hand on Sir William's shoulder.

"Do not worry, *mon ami*. We will find who did this. It is my promise."

Uh oh, thought PC Lucy, who'd experienced Chef Maurice's first attempts at impromptu sleuthing earlier that year.

He just said 'we'.

Back in the Bourne Hall kitchens, Mrs Bates was serving up cold beef sandwiches from the remains of what would have been the evening's dinner.

Chef Maurice would have preferred the slices a little pinker, but he allowed that Mrs Bates had suffered quite a shock today, and in her defence, the horseradish cream was both excellent and liberally applied.

PC Lucy entered the kitchen with a small police radio in her hand.

"My colleagues will be here shortly," she said. "In the meantime, if you wouldn't mind, Mr Gilles, I'd like to ask you some questions about Sir William?"

"Of course, madam," said Gilles, who'd been standing by the door, holding a cup of tea in the awkward manner of a man unaccustomed to social gatherings. He seemed quite relieved as he led PC Lucy down the hallway into Sir William's study.

It was a good-sized room, decorated to male tastes, with old oil paintings on the walls depicting historic battles, an abundance of oak panelling, and several firm, leather-studded armchairs.

"Are you certain you wouldn't prefer this interview to be conducted in private?" said PC Lucy, throwing an exasperated glance at Chef Maurice and Arthur, who'd followed them in and had settled themselves into the two armchairs by the small fireplace.

Gilles folded his hands neatly before him. "If the gentlemen wish to be present, I certainly have no objection. There is nothing I can tell you that would be in any way inappropriate."

"As you wish," said PC Lucy. "So walk me through the events of this evening."

Gilles cleared his throat. "From which point in the evening would you like me to start?"

"How about when you last saw Sir William?"

"I last saw Sir William at around seven o'clock, when he was entertaining the guests in the main drawing room. I poured the Champagne, then stepped into the dining room to check on the table arrangements. I heard Sir William leave the drawing room to go collect the final wines from the cellar, accompanied by Mr Paloni. I remained in the drawing room, where I was joined by Mr Wordington-Smythe and Mr Manchot. It was here that Mrs Bates found us and informed us that Sir William was apparently locked in the cellar and not responding. We then proceeded at once to the cellar entrance to lend assistance."

PC Lucy nodded as she scribbled in her notebook. "So the other guests were still in the drawing room?"

"No. Only Lady Margaret, who I believe was resting by the fire. The other guests had retired upstairs at that point."

"And then?"

"On finding the door to the cellar locked, as per Mrs Bates' description, and not being able to rouse a response from Sir William, I came here to the study to procure the spare key from the safe." He gestured towards the wall by the desk, where a small iron safe was embedded at chest height.

"May I see inside?"

"Of course." Gilles walked over to the safe and twiddled the dial. The little door swung open.

The safe was mostly empty, save for a bottle of forty-year-old single malt whisky—"Worth a pretty penny!" whispered Arthur—and a small pile of papers.

"As you can see," said Gilles, "Sir William was not in the habit of making much use of the safe."

"But he kept the spare cellar key in here? Sealed in wax?"

"Yes, it was a practice he inherited from his father, I'm told, to ensure he knew exactly who had access to the cellar at any one time."

"So the only cellar key that could have been used to lock him in was the one that Sir William carried himself?"

"So it appears."

"Interesting. Carry on. So you went to fetch the spare key?"

"Yes. I then proceeded to unlock the cellar door, and descended first, followed by the guests, which in hindsight I am most regretful of. For the ladies and gentlemen to have to witness such a sight . . . " Gilles shook his head.

"Was it normal for Sir William to lock the cellar door when he was down there?"

"No, I'd say not. On rare occasions when he did not wish to be disturbed, perhaps."

"I understand that there had been some form of disagreement between him and Mr Paloni, just beforehand. Is it possible he locked the door after Mr Paloni had left him, to ensure he wouldn't be disturbed further?"

"Possible, yes."

"And what about the cellar itself? Is anything missing?"

"I would need to consult the cellar book and carry out a full audit to ascertain this. But the most valuable bottles in the collection are kept in a glass cabinet with a key code lock. I observed at the time that these bottles were undisturbed."

PC Lucy scribbled this down in her notebook. "And then what happened after?"

"To ensure the safety of the guests, I conducted a preliminary search of the building, and soon after discovered a broken window in the storeroom beside the kitchen. We concluded that this was where the intruder had entered and exited the premises."

"So this was before you called the police?"

"Yes. As our phone line has been non-functional since the afternoon, Mr Lafoute and I then walked to the main road to make the call."

Chef Maurice leaned over to Arthur. "The phone line, I find this most suspicious," he murmured. Arthur nodded his agreement.

"Have you worked for Sir William very long?"

"Fifteen years."

"And to your knowledge, has Sir William ever received any threats? Notes, phone calls, that kind of thing?"

Gilles smiled faintly. "The local pro-fox-hunting lobby have been known to send the occasional sternly worded letter, but no, nothing of a genuinely threatening nature. As far as I am aware, of course."

"What about past burglaries? I understand the wine collection is worth millions of pounds."

"Most certainly. Especially with the additions to the collection over the last five years. But we have never had any trouble here. Our location is fairly remote, and Sir William had a new security door installed over the summer, though more for insurance purposes, I'm given to understand, than due to any real apprehension of theft."

"And what about his . . . personal relationships?"

"Relationships?"

"Was there anyone Sir William was involved with? Romantically, I mean?"

Gilles appeared to blanch at this thought. "None whatsoever. Rightly or wrongly, I do believe Sir William regarded himself quite past the age of acquiring . . . a female companion, shall we say."

Chef Maurice made a sudden harrumphing sound, causing PC Lucy to shoot him a warning look.

"And how would you describe the relationship between Sir William and Mrs Ariane Lafoute?"

Gilles paused a moment, then answered: "They were acquainted through Mrs Lafoute's husband, Mr Bertie Lafoute, who has been known to Sir William for all his life, I understand, and has been a frequent guest here at Bourne Hall. As for Mrs Lafoute herself, I believe Sir William has only met her on a handful of occasions since their wedding two years ago."

There was a knock on the door, and a freckle-faced young man stuck his head in. He was wearing a police hat and a very long woolly scarf.

"Um, do you have a moment? It's a bit urgent," he said to PC Lucy, who nodded and gestured him in.

Chef Maurice brightened up. He'd encountered PC Alistair on a few previous occasions, and found him to be a very pleasant, honest young man who held his elders in great respect—unlike PC Lucy, who seemed to carry certain misguided views on what information Chef Maurice should and should not have access to. Thankfully, her colleague Alistair seemed to have no such shortcomings to *his* cheery personality.

"Um . . . " said PC Alistair, looking at Gilles.

"This is Mr Gilles, Sir William's butler. So what have you found?"

"The cellar is just how you described. Most of the team is still down there. But I've just been for a walk around the building and, well, the footprints just don't work out. You can see everything very clearly, you see, what with all the snow."

"What do you mean, they don't work out?" said PC Lucy.

"Well, there's two sets going up to the main gate and back, fairly recently—"

"Monsieur Gilles and Monsieur Lafoute," said Chef Maurice, nodding.

"—and then there's quite a lot of sets outside the side door to the east wing—"

"Yes, that's where I arrived, like I explained earlier," said PC Lucy quickly, shooting another look at Chef Maurice and Arthur. Clearly, the mysterious blond man was not yet a tale for general consumption. "And then?"

"That's it, miss. There's no other prints."

"None from the storeroom near the kitchen?" said PC Lucy sharply.

"It's clean snow all around, miss."

"But there was glass on the floor—" started Gilles.

"Could have been done earlier, sir. Or even a few days ago. The room doesn't look much used."

Gilles looked at PC Lucy. "I was in there this morning, just before lunchtime. I can assure you there was no sign of a break-in then."

"So it happened this afternoon, then," said PC Lucy. "The intruder could have been waiting in there—"

"Bah! With no footprints outside after? Do you see? It is *une ruse*. To take us away from the scent," said Chef Maurice.

"There's another thing, miss. The phone line was definitely cut on purpose. Halfway up the wire, where it runs outside."

"But I thought you said there were no other prints."

"That's right. So it must have been done earlier in the day, before the snow. But another thing, that bit of wire goes right outside the window of one of the parlour rooms on the west side."

"So it could have been cut by someone inside the house? Leaning out of the window?" said PC Lucy, her eyes on Gilles, who looked back at her impassively.

"Looks like it, miss."

PC Lucy shut her notebook and sighed. "I'll need to talk to each of the guests." She glared at Chef Maurice and Arthur. "In *private*. And if I catch you two listening at the door, I'll be making use of the cells tonight, I swear."

Chef Maurice stood up and bowed solemnly.

"We would not dream of it, *mademoiselle*."

Not when, he thought, he had much more fruitful plans for his evening. Though no one had voiced the thought out loud, the lack of footprints outside the broken window could only mean one thing.

The storeroom had only been a diversion, a clever trick that might have very well worked, if it hadn't been for the snow.

But now they knew that no one had entered, and no one had left.

Which meant the real killer was someone who had been in the house all along.

"Good of you to listen to Lucy for once," said Arthur to Chef Maurice, as they shut the study door behind them.

PC Alistair had disappeared off into the house, and Gilles had been dispatched to summon the first interviewee. "You do rather upset her sometimes."

"*Mon ami*, I have only the most high respect for Mademoiselle Lucy and her work."

"Is that so?"

"Yes. I am certain she will conduct the interviews with the most professional correctness. But the talking, this can be done anytime. The rooms, however . . . "

Arthur followed Chef Maurice as he hastened up the main staircase. A heavy door led to a landing of sorts, with a window at one end facing the front of the house. The only light source now was the dim glow of an ornate porcelain table lamp.

Sir William had once given Arthur the grand tour of the Hall. His own master bedroom, though the tour had not extended quite so far as to see inside, was the door at the far end of the corridor, flanked on one side by a large mahogany bookcase, laden with tomes spanning centuries, languages and genres, presumably thus placed to save insomniac guests from having to venture downstairs to the main library. There was also a small cut glass decanter of what smelled like brandy and some square glasses.

Sir William had been a most genial host, indeed.

The other doors all led to the various guest rooms.

They located PC Alistair across the hallway, in the suite occupied by Bertie and Ariane.

"Does PC Gavistone know you're up here, sir?"

Chef Maurice drew himself up importantly. "I informed Mademoiselle Lucy that we were most ready to aid her in this investigation as much as possible."

While PC Alistair considered this statement, Chef Maurice took the chance to duck past him into the room and subject its contents to a thoroughly good staring, hands on hips.

This stage completed, he looked over at PC Alistair. "So where do we begin?"

There were two travel suitcases leaned up against the wall, neither of which contained anything of much interest, save for a rather large amount of silk and lace in Ariane's that turned PC Alistair's ears a bashful shade of pink.

They migrated into the en-suite bathroom, where his-and-hers toiletries were lined up either side of the double sink like two opposing armies. A peek into a capacious satin-lined vanity case revealed that Ariane shared the usual hypochondriac tendencies of many of her countrymen, and travelled with a vast array of painkillers, anti-nausea tablets, sleeping pills, stomach pastilles, flu remedies, and all the other items necessary to set up a fully operating pharmacy wherever your travels took you.

Over at the writing desk, Chef Maurice unrolled a large architectural drawing. "*Très impressionant.*"

"Is it a plan of Bourne Hall?" said PC Alistair. He had been expounding his theories on the existence of a secret underground passageway that would allow a nefarious outsider to enter and exit the building unseen—the young policeman being uncomfortable with the thought of any of the fine upstanding citizens downstairs being potential murderers—and was keen to be proved correct.

Chef Maurice shook his head and pointed to the building in the centre of the map. "It is a plan of Chateau Lafoute. And this new building, it appears to be a winery."

Arthur whistled. "Not just a winery. Look, they're planning a visitor centre too. Very spacious. Looks like a serious undertaking. Do you think Sir William was going to be one of their investors?"

"If he was, it would give Monsieur Bertie and Madame Ariane a reason for *not* wishing his murder."

"Very true."

They exited the suite and moved on to Resnick's room next door. The decor was decidedly more spartan, with a four-poster oak bed, a desk and wardrobe and sombre maroon wallpaper. On the bedside table was a pile of blue-backed notebooks—"He claims to record every single wine he drinks," sniffed Arthur—as well as a few brochures from recent wine auctions.

Resnick's cat-hair-ravaged clothes were hung on the back of the door, and they found a selection of fresh shirts and trousers arranged in the wardrobe. Aside from the usual travel necessities, a search of his suitcase revealed a small flask of whisky, a half-eaten jar of potted mackerel, and a box of crackers.

"He is a more sensible man than I thought," said Chef Maurice in tones of approval.

Next up was Lady Margaret's room, which, compared to the last two rooms, had a much more lived-in feel. Clearly this was her regular abode when visiting her brother-in-law.

"Do you really think one of the guests did it?" said Arthur, as he flicked through the stack of hardback novels on the nightstand. "Hard to imagine any of this lot smashing a bottle over anyone's head, let alone going for the throat afterwards."

"A murderer can come from the most unexpected places," said Chef Maurice, staring sternly at Lady Margaret's lacy-cuffed rose-patterned bathrobe.

There was the sound of glassware rolling across tiles. "Whoops," came PC Alistair's voice from the bathroom.

They found him on his knees, scrabbling on the floor for a wayward jar that had escaped from a battered embroidered carry bag containing a collection of creams, lotions and ointments, all giving off an overly floral scent. There were tubs of '100% natural' remedies, various herb-based lozenges, and several phials of 'aroma-centric calming oils'.

"Just as well Sir William wasn't poisoned," said Arthur to PC Alistair. "Your labs would be tied up for weeks with all this lot. And Ariane's collection too."

Paloni had somehow managed to snag the most opulent of the guest suites. Every piece of furniture was upholstered in thick gold-threaded brocade, the bed linen felt like silk, and the bathroom was dominated by an elegant claw-foot bath.

"*Très* 'Ollywood," commented Chef Maurice.

The wet loofah and half-empty bottle of expensive bubble bath suggested that Paloni had wasted no time in availing himself of the amenities on offer.

"What kind of gentleman wears red silk boxers?" demanded Arthur, recoiling from the suitcase that PC Alistair had just popped open. "*And* carries around signed photographs of himself," he added, as PC Alistair used a pen to push aside the offending undergarments, revealing a stack of prints beneath.

"There was once a lady in the restaurant, she expressed herself as a fan of your restaurant column. She even carried a picture of you in her wallet," said Chef Maurice, rummaging through the wardrobe.

"What? Where'd she get a picture of me?"

"She cut it from the newspaper, I think."

"But they haven't changed that photo for decades!"

"*Oui*. I told the lady she would be most disappointed if she should meet you now."

A worrying thought crept across Arthur's mind. "You didn't tell Meryl about this, did you? She gets jealous over the smallest of things," he said, nevertheless with a smidgen of pride regarding his status as an evidently much-coveted male.

"*Oui*, of course I tell her. But do not worry, she found it to be most amusing."

"Hmph," said Arthur, manly pride somewhat deflated.

They also found various letters and financial papers relating to Paloni's wine venture, the Basking Buffalo winery. There were several iterations of the agenda for the upcoming shareholders' meeting in two weeks' time. In the latest, Sir William's listing as the after-dinner speaker had been crossed out. With some force.

"Interesting," murmured Arthur. The accompanying Annual Report also bore further scrutiny, littered as it was with telling phrases such as 'rising to the inevitable challenges', 'longer-term site potential' and 'much appreciated continuing support of our shareholders'. All was not well at Basking Buffalo.

"Cash flow troubles, if you read between the lines," said Arthur, handing the report to Chef Maurice, who flipped through, looking at the glossy pictures.

"And we know that Sir William was an investor."

"Or so Paloni told us," said Arthur, thinking about the crossed-out agenda.

The guest rooms dealt with, PC Alistair led the way up to the attic rooms, where Gilles and Mrs Bates had their living quarters.

Mrs Bates' rooms were functional and spotlessly clean, bare of personal memorabilia apart from a half-eaten box of milk chocolates and a small shelf of well-thumbed paperbacks featuring smouldering-looking young men wearing top hats and waistcoats, and frilly ladies in horse-drawn carriages.

Gilles's quarters consisted of two rooms: a living room and a smaller bedroom. The former afforded him a small fireplace, an armchair and a desk, while the latter housed a single bed and a wardrobe almost entirely filled with white shirts, pressed black trousers, and a row of identical tailcoats. A stool and shoeshine kit were neatly arranged in one corner.

PC Alistair set about peering behind furniture and riffling through the drawers, with the desperate enthusiasm of one who has failed to find anything suitably incriminating to report back to one's superiors.

Thankfully for the young policeman, Chef Maurice's excavations under the bed revealed a strange metal suitcase, about the size of two briefcases put together. He laid it on the bed and reached for the fastenings.

"Wait, it might be a bomb," said Arthur.

"Bah, who will sleep with a bomb under their bed?" said Chef Maurice and snapped open the locks. "*Voilà!*"

Two very old, and most likely highly valuable, bottles of wine stared back up at them, nestled quietly in the black velvet interior. A small thermometer monitored their temperature, and the whole case hummed gently as the thermostat kicked into action.

"A 1918 Cheval Blanc and 1945 Mouton," said Arthur. "Not a butler's usual bedtime drink, I should think."

It appeared to be time for another little chat with Gilles.

CHAPTER 8

In the kitchens of Le Cochon Rouge, the big clock over the prep station ticked its way past two o'clock in the morning. Chef Maurice stood at the stove, stirring a pot of thick hot chocolate.

They'd returned to find Alf fast asleep on the floor, arms and legs wrapped firmly around a sack of potatoes. Patrick had loaded the commis chef into a handy wheelbarrow, spuds and all, covered him with a blanket and headed down into Beakley to deliver Alf to his lodgings.

"So, you believe the explanation of Monsieur Gilles?" said Chef Maurice, thumping three full mugs down on the table.

PC Lucy shrugged. "I don't have any reason not to."

"Bah! 'Taking wines for a valuation'? Why does the company not come to the Hall? *Non*, I tell you, Monsieur Gilles, he keeps the truth hidden. I have many suspicions."

"You always have suspicions," said Arthur, who was leaning back in his chair, eyes closed.

"And is it not true that, very often, it is the butler who did it?"

"Only in the movies, Maurice."

"And anyway," said PC Lucy, "you told me Gilles was in the dining room the whole time with you and Arthur. He *can't* be the murderer."

"Hmph," said Chef Maurice, miffed at having provided the dubious bottle-borrowing butler with such a cast-iron alibi.

"Well, it wasn't me or Maurice. And unless dear old Mrs Bates had finally had enough of making mini Yorkshire puds—"

"*Non, non*, she is too short. Sir William, he was hit on the head, *n'est-ce pas*?"

PC Lucy nodded. "Pretty hard, too."

"All right, so unless Mrs Bates carried a stool down into the cellar with her, we're left with our five guests," said Arthur.

"Plus we still don't have an explanation for how the cellar door came to be locked in the first place," said PC Lucy, "with the key left in Sir William's pocket."

"And do not forget, too, the man in black who made an attack on Patrick," said Chef Maurice.

"In all fairness, it sounded more like he was simply trying to get away from *you*, Maurice," said Arthur. "Patrick was just in the wrong place at the wrong time."

"Hmph, still, a man appearing at the Hall on the same night as a murder must be considered most suspicious, I think."

"We know it can't have been him, though," said PC Lucy. "Patrick and I followed him all the way over there, and he'd been in the restaurant the whole afternoon, according to Alf."

"And he only ordered one dish," sniffed Chef Maurice, studying the order tickets.

"At least he paid his bill. And he tipped," Arthur pointed out. They'd found the money earlier on the table, in crisp twenty-pound notes.

"Who treks across the middle of nowhere with a gun in a briefcase, runs away when we try to stop him, and *still* pays for his dinner?" said PC Lucy, who was looking quite frazzled by the night's events.

"*Oui*, a most polite criminal, it seems."

The front door banged as Patrick came in, wheelbarrow hefted in one hand. (Chef Maurice could be very particular when it came to the dining room floor.)

"Sleeping like the dead," he reported. "But don't worry, chef, I set him five alarm clocks. And hid two of them. He'll be here tomorrow morning, all right."

Chef Maurice nodded in satisfaction. He had firm views on punctuality, as long as they didn't apply to him, of course.

"Today morning, in fact," said Arthur, looking up at the clock and stretching his arms. "I'd better be getting on home."

"Me too," said PC Lucy, standing up. "I have a feeling tomorrow's going to be a busy day."

"I'll walk you home," said Patrick quickly.

Chef Maurice, left alone in the kitchens, ran the tap over the empty hot chocolate pan, and stared out of the window into the dark night. Moonlight picked out tendrils of frost as they crept around the edges of the panes.

First thing tomorrow, he decided, he would pay a return visit to Bourne Hall. There were still far too many unanswered questions for his liking. But first, a good night's sleep was in order.

He glanced out of the window again. It was definitely hot-water bottle weather.

Except that Chef Maurice's own hot-water bottle was of a rather unique construction, complete with a special lining that allowed it to be filled with any beverage of his choice.

That way, if he got thirsty in the middle of the night, there'd be a nice hot drink ready to keep him company.

Tonight, he plumped for the spiced mulled cider.

Thus amply provisioned, he slipped the rubber bottle into its fluffy cover, and mounted the stairs to bed.

The snow had turned the village green into a giant square of frosted icing—that was, apart from the faux Vauxhall Astra and the recent appearance of a line of snowmen doing the conga.

Patrick stamped his feet as PC Lucy patted her pockets for her keys.

"You don't have to wait for me, you know," she said.

"I know." He drew a deep breath, the icy air stinging his tongue. "Um, do you have plans for Sunday dinner? I'm pretty sure I can get the evening shift off."

"Oh." She looked rather startled. "I'm afraid I can't. I'm meeting a friend for dinner."

Patrick felt his stomach tighten. Had there been a slight hesitation in her voice? "In Beakley?"

"No, um, over in Cowton. But how about the Tuesday evening after? We could go see the Christmas lights go on in Endleby. No naked men, I promise you."

She smiled, and tiptoed up to kiss him on the lips.

"I'm not sure I can make the same promise," he said, wrapping his arms around her waist and attempting what he hoped was a roguish grin.

PC Lucy rolled her eyes and swatted his arm. "Nice try. You go get some sleep." She brushed her lips past his again, then disappeared inside.

Patrick trudged back past the green. Surely Alf must have been mistaken. After all, there were surely dozens, even hundreds, of blonde women living in Cowton. Statistically, at least a few of them had to bear a passing resemblance to PC Lucy.

But then, if it *wasn't* a mistake . . .

He walked on.

What he needed now was a way to be *sure*.

The next morning at Le Cochon Rouge, any plans for sleuthing had to be put temporarily on hold, after a

91

distraught telephone call from a table of twelve, whose Christmas lunch at another restaurant had just been cancelled due to a night-time break-in.

"*C'est terrible!*" announced Chef Maurice to the rest of the kitchen, after he put the phone down. "The thieves, they stole every turkey! And ten kilos of Camembert! It is *incroyable* what these people will steal."

"Speaking of turkeys, chef," said Patrick, as he pulled out more trays to prep the extra ingredients for their sudden lunchtime additions, "we still don't have a main dish sorted for the Elmore Society Christmas Dinner next Monday. You said you were going to arrange something?"

Chef Maurice tapped his nose. "Do not worry. It is under my control."

The next few hours were spent devising and preparing an impromptu five-course lunch for their beleaguered new guests. A dill-and-beetroot-cured salmon fillet was fetched from the walk-in, its firm flesh ready for slicing, and a dozen confit duck legs were dug out of a big tub of solid seasoned fat.

Alf, with dark rings under his eyes and the shattered nerves of someone operating on a quadruple dose of strong black coffee, was set to work breaking up a pile of thick chocolate squares and zesting a box of oranges for the chocolate-and-orange fondants.

Situation now under control, Chef Maurice poured another shot of espresso into Alf's mug, then headed into Beakley towards the Wordington-Smythe cottage.

Like many men in possession of a good fortune, Arthur had long succeeded in fulfilling his want for a wife. Meryl, however, as a woman in possession of a man of good fortune, was still working her way through *her* list of wants, but the latest had resulted in the purchase of a four-by-four bewheeled monstrosity, suitable for navigating Arctic tundra, dense jungles and, as it turned out, snowy Cotswold villages.

"It's not like we live in the middle of the Highlands," grumbled Arthur, as he pulled out of his drive with Chef Maurice in the passenger seat. "Still, I suppose it does have its uses," he said, as they crunched their way past a neighbour sat in his two-seater, pounding the steering wheel, wheels spinning ineffectually against the snow.

Chef Maurice, who was busy fiddling with all the heated-seat controls, nodded and gave the dashboard a little pat.

"It is a good car. Meryl has fine taste. See, there is even a space for my coffee," he said, pointing to the extra-large thermos in the holder beside him.

Gilles opened the front door just as they pulled up.

"Good morning, sirs," he said, though his face belied the fact that this was anything but a good morning.

"We are here to see Monsieur and Madame Lafoute, Monsieur Paloni, Monsieur Resnick and Lady Margaret."

"I'm afraid, sir, that Lady Margaret already left first thing this morning, and Mr Resnick departed an hour ago to return to London."

"Sign of a guilty conscience, no doubt," muttered Arthur.

"But the other two gentlemen are currently taking lunch in the Morning Room, if you would care to join them. I understand Mrs Lafoute is still feeling the effects of yesterday's events and has chosen to remain in her room. Do not alarm yourself, I instructed Mrs Bates to take her up a tray," he added, correctly interpreting Chef Maurice's look of concern.

In the Morning Room, the drapes had been pulled back to let cold white light into the high-ceilinged room. The two male guests were sitting in awkward silence over plates of hot-smoked salmon served with a leek-and-potato soup. Paloni in particular looked relieved at the sight of the new visitors.

"Morning, fellas! I would say good morning, but that'd be a darn lie, of course. Come and dig in. That lady Mrs Bates thinks we've got four stomachs each, the amount she's gone and cooked."

"And how is Madame Ariane?" said Chef Maurice to Bertie.

"Not the best, I'm afraid," said Bertie, who looked rather worse for wear himself. "But definitely better now, compared to last night. She got herself quite worked up, hardly slept all night. Only dropped off around eight this morning."

"She's one of those sensitive types," said Paloni, waving his fork. "See it a lot with actresses. Perfectly poised, most of the time, and then one little thing sets them off—"

"I think Uncle William being murdered is more than 'one little thing'," said Bertie stiffly.

"'Course, 'course, didn't mean it like that," said Paloni, throwing Chef Maurice one of those 'the English, aren't they a funny lot' looks.

"How long are you both staying here?" asked Arthur, helping himself to a cup of tea while Chef Maurice tackled the chafing dish of hot-smoked salmon.

"My driver's on his way down," said Paloni. "Traffic getting out of London was a killer, at least that's what he tells me, but he should be here soon. I'm giving these folks a ride back too, if the lady can manage it, of course."

"The police, have they come again?" asked Chef Maurice.

Bertie shook his head.

"They took down all our details last night. Passports, hotels, all that jazz," said Paloni, looking offended.

"They obviously think it was one of us," said Bertie, in matter-of-fact tones.

"Well, I'll be contacting my embassy if any more of those cops turn up, trying to make out I had anything to do with it. Couldn't find the guy that did it, so now they're trying to pin it on one of us. I mean, we were all upstairs. What do they think we are, the Invisible Man? You saw me"—he turned to Bertie—"didn't ya, coming out of my room?"

Bertie nodded, though a tad reluctantly.

"And I saw you just about to run down those stairs. And your lady and that wine fella, they must have come down not a minute after us."

"But, Lady Margaret, she was not upstairs," Chef Maurice pointed out, causing Paloni to let out a great guffaw.

"Now you're really scraping the barrel, my friend, if you're telling me that pipe cleaner of a woman had anything to do with it! I mean, she could hardly keep her eyes open—"

He stopped, with a guilty look, as Gilles glided into the room and addressed him.

"Sir, your car from London has arrived."

"Right about time, too," said Paloni, jumping up. "Enjoy your lunch," he said, nodding at Chef Maurice and Arthur, and hightailed out of the room.

Bertie folded his napkin on his plate and stood up. "I better go and make sure Ariane is ready." He shook their hands solemnly. "I'm sorry we didn't have a chance to meet under better circumstances."

"Likewise," said Arthur.

"Can I get you gentlemen anything else?" said Gilles, watching Chef Maurice upturn the remains of the lemon hollandaise over his plate.

"*Oui*. I would be most interested if you will recount for me the events of yesterday. Not the evening, which we all know, but from the morning. How was the *tempérament* of Sir William? Did anything happen that was not usual?"

Gilles pursed his lips, but replied, "Nothing unusual that I recall. Sir William rose at eight, as was his routine, and took breakfast here in the Morning Room. He then spent the rest of the day attending to various private matters in his study, though he took lunch in the dining room with Mr and Mrs Lafoute and Mr Paloni, who arrived at around midday from London."

"At what time did the other guests arrive?"

"Lady Margaret arrived just after three, I believe, and Mr Resnick not long after her."

"Did Sir William come out to greet his guests?"

"Yes. He came out and spoke briefly with Lady Margaret. And he spoke to Mr Resnick for quite some time in his study."

"Do you know what it is they discussed?"

"I would not have dreamed of enquiring," said Gilles, looking mildly shocked. "But one might surmise their conversation pertained to Sir William's various wine investments. Mr Resnick has been a frequent guest here in recent years, advising Sir William on his various purchases."

"What about the other guests?" asked Arthur. "What did they do the whole afternoon while Sir William was holed up in his study?"

"I'm afraid I cannot account for the entirety of our guests' movements that afternoon, nor would I wish to do so. I know that Mr and Mrs Lafoute took a turn around the gardens in the mid-afternoon, before the snow started, only because Sir William asked me to fetch Mrs

Lafoute to his study to speak with him. I believe he had some enquiries about the history of Chateau Lafoute, in preparation for the evening's tasting."

"When was this?" asked Arthur.

"Sometime before three, I remember, as it was before Lady Margaret arrived. But as to the rest of the afternoon, I'm afraid I was quite occupied with preparations for the evening's dinner and attending to the wines that were to be served."

Chef Maurice looked up from wiping his plate clean with a slice of bread. "You went down into the cellar, then? With the use of Sir William's key?"

"Yes. This was our usual routine. Sir William had already laid out the bottles several days ago. I merely brought them upstairs to allow them to come to serving temperature for the evening."

"And did you notice anything different in the cellar?"

"Nothing that drew my attention, sir. Everything was exactly as it should have been."

"So apart from talking to Resnick and Mrs Lafoute, Sir William was alone in his study for the whole afternoon?" asked Arthur. "Did he take any calls, or receive any other visitors?"

"Certainly no calls. The line rings first on the hallway phone, so I would be the one to receive any incoming calls before putting them through."

"And visitors? Or his guests?" said Chef Maurice, watching the butler's face.

Gilles hesitated. "It was the early evening and I was in the hallway—I remember because this was when I first discovered that the phone line was down—when Lady Margaret came downstairs and insisted on speaking to Sir William. I informed her that the master had specifically asked not to be disturbed, but she was not, shall we say, amenable to that suggestion. Short of restraining her, there was little I could do."

"When exactly was this?" said Arthur.

"Around five o'clock, I believe."

"Before or after he spoke to Resnick?"

"After," said Gilles promptly. "And before you ask me, sir, no, I do not know what Lady Margaret wished to speak to Sir William about."

"Did she say anything to you after?" asked Chef Maurice.

Gilles coughed. He seemed unwilling to tell a direct lie, and it was obvious that this interrogation was paining him. "Lady Margaret did say something to me afterwards, on the lines of how she considered herself an excellent judge of character, especially in regards to a certain guest. I did not enquire as to the person she was referring to, but she seemed quite satisfied with the outcome of her meeting."

"I see," murmured Chef Maurice.

"Seems that for a man who didn't want to be disturbed, Sir William had quite a few little chats that afternoon," said Arthur.

"So it appears." Gilles cleared his throat once more. "If that will be all, sirs?"

"One final thing, Monsieur Gilles. May we go to speak with Madame Bates?"

Surprisingly, Gilles looked quite gratified by this suggestion.

"Yes, of course. If you would follow me. If I might say, sir, I believe it would be of great help for Mrs Bates to have someone to talk to."

"How is she doing?" said Arthur. "I mean, this can hardly be the easiest of circumstances. I understand she's been here even longer than you have."

Gilles, always the good servant, hesitated.

"Perhaps, sir, you should see for yourself."

The Bourne Hall kitchens looked as if half a dozen pastry chefs had moved in and proceeded to start a competitive bake-off.

Every surface was covered in bags of flour, cartons of eggs, wooden spoons, whisks and mixing bowls of all designs and sizes. The central table was home to a three-tier black forest gateau, a large chocolate brownie cake, one rotund Christmas pudding, a wedding-style square white cake encrusted in icing swirls, dozens of home-made mince pies, and a trio of cream-and-fruit-loaded pavlovas. The smell of fresh jam bubbling on the stove heralded the imminent arrival of at least a quartet of Victoria sponge cakes.

Waffles the grey Persian was meandering around under the table, her paws white with flour, blinking up at the creamy delights and biding her time.

Chef Maurice, who had experienced his fair share of cooks in the midst of an emotional crisis, carefully edged his way up next to Mrs Bates.

"Tell me what can I do, Madame Bates?"

"The cream needs whipping, and I need you to go check on the oatmeal-and-raisin cookies in the second oven. And make sure the jam isn't setting too firm." Mrs Bates kept her eyes firmly fixed on the sponge cakes as she eased them out of their shallow tins.

"*Oui*, at once, *madame*."

Silently, working in tandem and watched by Arthur and Waffles, they assembled the four Victoria sponges and dusted them with icing sugar.

As Mrs Bates reached for another bag of flour, Chef Maurice quickly took her hand and patted it. "Perhaps it is time for a cup of tea, Madame Bates?"

She looked up at him, as if noticing his presence for the first time.

"Deary me, Mister Maurice, of course, how rude of me. Oh, and Mister Arthur too. Do have a seat. Sugar, milk?"

"Three sugars and milk, *merci*."

"Just a dash of milk for me, thanks."

Mrs Bates bustled around the kitchen, trailed by Waffles, who had recognised the word 'milk'.

"Horrible, simply horrible," muttered Mrs Bates.

Chef Maurice and Arthur nodded along in sympathy.

"And down in his own wine cellar too. He loved that place, I tell you, spent a near fortune on it, what with all the whizzy doors and fancy locks. Always thought, if we were ever under attack, it'd be straight down into those cellars, safest place in the house. Waffles even had her kittens down there last spring, disappeared one day and then next thing we know, we're on our hands and knees looking under crates and all. Dearest little things, they all found a good home too, bless 'em."

"Under attack, did you say?" said Arthur. "Was Sir William ever threatened in some way?"

"Oh no, that was just a figure of speech, Mister Arthur. He was a gentle man, the master was, never could stand to quarrel. Wouldn't hurt a fly, and I mean it. He'd have Gilles trap 'em in a glass and let 'em outside. Wouldn't raise a finger, not to man or beast. I remember those fox hunting people, coming round causing a fuss. We had a whole family of them, the foxes, I mean, cubs and all, bless 'em, living out by the greenhouses. And why not? We don't keep chickens, they were no trouble to us."

"Was Sir William in any way different, in this last week or month?" said Chef Maurice.

Mrs Bates filled the kettle and stood tapping her foot. "He hadn't been himself lately, that's for certain," she said finally.

"Really?" said Arthur. "How so?"

"Kept going on about trust and betrayal. And how you never really know a person . . . "

"Did he mention any names?"

"No, and I never would've asked, of course."

"Could he have been talking about one of the guests who were here yesterday? Do you think he was acting differently to any of them?"

"I really couldn't say. I was in here most of the day, you see, sorting out their lunch, and then the big dinner, of course. He didn't even think to tell us he was coming for lunch, that American film fellow, and bringing Bertie and his lady wife too. If I hadn't just happened to have that steak-and-ale pie all ready in the pantry, it would have been a disaster, mark my words. Sometimes I reckon they think I work some kind of magic in here."

Chef Maurice nodded understandingly, while surreptitiously sliding a hot oatmeal cookie off the tray.

"Do you know much about the guests?" asked Arthur. "Was there any ill feeling between any of them and Sir William, as far as you know?"

"Now, that's a silly question. They wouldn't have been invited here if there was," said Mrs Bates, tutting. "As for knowing them, well, let's see. Lady Margaret's been coming to visit ever since I worked here, and that's nigh on twenty-five years now. Of course, she used to come with her husband, spitting image of Sir William, he was, just a bit older, and their little boy. Though he's all grown up now, of course. She likes her sweets, she does, but gives me ever such an earful if I leave too much fat on the roasts. Flavour's in the fats, I try to tell her, but she won't listen. Set in her ways, she is."

"I have the same complaint at my restaurant sometimes," said Chef Maurice, spreading jam onto the cookie.

"But I make compensation by using the extra fat on the roast potatoes. Some of my customers, they tell me they drive two hours for my roast potatoes."

"And the other guests?" said Arthur, keen to get the conversation back on a less cholesterol-heavy track.

"Now, Mister Bertie, he's been coming to the Hall ever since he was a babe! Used to run all around the kitchens, looking for hiding holes. Found him in amongst the pots and pans, more than once. Such a sad story, his poor parents. You know they died in a car crash? Mister Bertie would've been with them, too, except he was laid up with flu that day. Only sixteen, he was."

"A tale most *tragique*. And what of Madame Ariane? Did Sir William approve of Monsieur Bertie's choice in a wife?"

"Hah, like approval's got anything to do with it, what with 'em young people these days. Funny you should say that though, Mister Maurice. I always thought the master was a bit, well, reserved when it came to Mrs Lafoute. You could see him holding back judgement, like. I always reckoned he thought she wasn't good enough for Mister Bertie. And what a thought! A bit high-minded, I'll give you that, but she's a real lady, Mrs Lafoute is. Anyone can see that."

"Perhaps," said Chef Maurice, thinking about the note they'd found in Sir William's pocket. "And what is your impression of Monsieur Paloni and Monsieur Resnick?"

"Oh, I was in a right tizzy, I was, having a movie star

up here at the Hall. He did put me out, though, when he turned up out of the blue for lunch like that, but golly if he ain't a handsome fellow! He knows it too, though you can't really blame him. And his teeth! Whiter than an angel's laundry line, I'll tell you."

"He had come here before?"

"Oh no, never. You know, I rather fancy he invited himself up, the way the master put it. Told me last week we'd be having an extra guest to stay, and the way he said it made me think he was none too pleased."

"Ah, so there was bad feeling between Sir William and Monsieur Paloni?"

"Oh, hardly like that. Sir William loves to host a big party, and he was soon all excited again, saying it'd be just like Paris or something, having a big dinner with the Americans against the French."

"What about Resnick?" asked Arthur. "I hear he's up here pretty often?"

"Oh yes, up here like clockwork, talking Sir William into buying all those fancy old bottles that nobody ever drinks. I told the master, you can't take it with you. I mean, it's good for a gentleman to have a hobby, keeps 'em out of mischief, but at the end of the day, wine's made for drinking. You don't see me collecting centuries' worth of jam jars in the pantry, just to ogle at, do you?"

"Quite," said Arthur.

Chef Maurice drained his teacup. "*Merci, madame.* You have given us much to think around. Now, we must continue on with our search." He reached over to the bell cord to summon Gilles.

"Continue on to where?" said Arthur.

"The cellar, of course. We must return to the scene of the crime."

"We must?" Arthur gave a little shudder.

"Can I get you gentlemen anything to eat before you go?" said Mrs Bates. "All this shock, plays havoc with the appetite, I tell you."

Chef Maurice surveyed the table, which was groaning with the cumulative weight of all the cakes.

"If you would be so kind, *madame*, I would most enjoy a kipper sandwich."

If Mrs Bates thought the request in any way odd, she was professional enough a cook not to show it. "Certainly, Mister Maurice, I'll just go see if we have any out the back."

"Clever," whispered Arthur, as Mrs Bates disappeared into the pantry. "Get her mind off the cakes. Can't think about dessert in a kitchen reeking of smoked fish."

"Ah, *mon ami*, once again you do not see," said Chef Maurice, helping himself to a still-warm mince pie.

"See what?" said Arthur indignantly.

"I am confident that soon we will solve the mystery of the locked cellar and the single brass key."

"With the help of a kipper sandwich?"

"*Oui.*"

Under the table, Waffles perked up. Someone had just mentioned kippers.

CHAPTER 9

Patrick put down the receiver and made a small cross on the piece of paper beside him.

"Three down, six to go," he announced to the dining room, which was empty apart from Dorothy, doing a stocktake behind the bar, and Alf, who was laid out on a bench taking a post-caffeine snooze.

"Are you sure you want to be doing this, luv?" asked Dorothy, as Patrick consulted his list for the next number.

"It's not a matter of want, it's a matter of must," replied Patrick grimly.

"Why don't you just hack into their booking systems?" suggested Alf, opening one eye.

Patrick, in his pre-cheffing days, had dabbled in a short-lived career as a software engineer, which, in Alf's eyes, meant that he commanded a range of godlike powers over all technological realms.

"First off, that's illegal, and secondly, if these places are anything like us"—Patrick held up Le Cochon Rouge's own bookings diary, its edges wavy from use and its pages liberally marked by Chef Maurice's coffee cup stains—"then I doubt they're hackable in the first place."

He dialled the next number. After a few moments, the line picked up and a light symphony of background chatter filtered through.

"Trattoria Bennucci," said the male voice at the other end of the line. "How may I help you?"

"Hi, I think my friend made us a booking for dinner on Sunday evening," said Patrick, his heart thumping, "but I can't remember what time she booked for. The table's under her name, I think. Gavistone."

There was the rustling of pages. Probably just for show, thought Patrick, to impress upon him how fully booked they were.

Trattoria Bennucci was one of the more pricey establishments in Cowton, with the type of clientele who were more concerned about the low-lit, faux-rustic decor, which served as an eminently suitable venue for prospective amorous encounters, than with the quality of food, which was cheap knock-off Italian, at best.

"Yeessss, Gavistone. Seven pee-em, for three people?"

"Three— Oh, yes, that's right. Seven o'clock. Great, thanks."

Patrick hung up, his heart heavy as an anvil.

"She booked a table for three," he reported. "At Trattoria Bennucci."

"There you go, then," said Dorothy, with a told-you-so smile. "She's just having dinner with friends, nothing to worry about."

"No, this is worse." A table for three meant that not only was Lucy having dinner with another man, she was bringing along a friend to meet her not-so-secret lover. He and Lucy had yet to proceed to the 'meeting each other's friends' stage. Which meant that—horror of horrors—*he* was the other man.

"You're catastrophising, luv," said Dorothy, reading his expression. "Making mountains out of molehills. You've nothing to go on. Just talk to her straight, you might just be surprised . . . "

But Patrick had stopped listening. He'd just had a thought. It was a bold, daring thought, with potential for things to go very wrong indeed.

But it was also a thought that might just win him PC Lucy's respect and undying love.

That was worth a shot, surely. But first, he'd need to go shopping.

They left Waffles mewing at the top of the stairs in a kipper-induced trance, and carefully shut the cellar door.

Gilles led the way down, the slight wrinkle of his nose indicating that he did not at all approve of letting Arthur and Chef Maurice poke their way around Bourne Hall, but had yet to find a suitably decorous manner in which to eject them from the building.

The nose wrinkling might also have been due to the large hot-smoked kipper sandwich that Chef Maurice was currently munching his way through, wrapped neatly in a white linen napkin by Mrs Bates.

"I still don't see what you need that sandwich for," whispered Arthur, as they bent down to examine the flagstones where Sir William had fallen. "You already had salmon for lunch."

The forensics team had removed all the shattered glass, but a few tiny fragments still glinted in the grooves between the stone slabs.

"Patience, *mon ami*."

"And you don't even like kippers."

"I learn to appreciate the taste."

"Hah. You gave half of it away to the cat."

Chef Maurice bent down to inspect a bottle on a lower shelf. "She was looking at me. What was I to do?"

Arthur decided to abandon this line of enquiry and conduct his own search of the crime scene.

He'd been down into the cellars before on previous visits, but had never quite taken in the full extent of Sir William's collection.

It wasn't a particularly large room, at least by wine-collecting standards, but every vertical surface had been put to use with a criss-cross grid of wooden shelves holding a vast array of bottles, all neatly stacked on their sides. There were fat heavy bottles of single-vineyard Chardonnays, rows of slim-necked German Rieslings, dark wax-encrusted bottles of vintage Port, and even the odd balthazar—the equivalent of sixteen normal bottles of wine in one gigantic glass behemoth, sufficient to serve a hundred guests, if you could find a waiter strong enough to lift it.

In one corner, a towering stack of wooden wine crates, each containing a dozen bottles and branded with various winery names, stood ready to take up their rightful place on the shelves.

Chef Maurice was now wandering up and down the rows, pulling out bottles at random and admiring their labels. Gilles followed him at a discreet distance, wiping the bottles down in fear of kipper contamination.

"Monsieur Gilles, tell me, what is the meaning of these dots of yellow?"

Arthur leaned in closer to the rack. Sure enough, here and there he could spot little round yellow stickers pressed to the bases of a seemingly arbitrary selection of bottles.

"I do not know, sir. Possibly Sir William was marking out wines to serve at future events."

Arthur pulled out the nearest yellow-stickered bottle. "An '82 Pétrus. Well, you can't deny that Sir William was a fantastically generous host."

He walked over to the display cabinet, which, in addition to the magnum collection, housed a dozen or so bottles from the much-fêted Burgundian vineyard, la Romanée Conti, along with various bottlings from a cult Californian wine producer with black circular labels apparently only legible under ultraviolet light.

There were quite a few yellow stickers on the magnums too, but, more importantly, there was now an extra empty podium in addition to the two blank places he'd noticed there yesterday.

"What happened to this one?" asked Arthur, pointing to the missing third exhibit. A little white card announced it as a magnum of '34 Chateau Ausone.

"Sir William had arranged for that particular bottle to be valued today, and I saw no reason to deviate from his wishes," said Gilles. "I would have taken it to London myself, as per usual, but due to obvious circumstances, I chose to remain here with our guests. A representative from the firm collected the bottle this morning."

"That's rather speedy," said Arthur.

"Not at all. There is an auction of fine and rare wines taking place at Sotheby's next week. Sir William had wished to have an estimation before considering whether to place the bottle up for sale. Of course, this will no longer go ahead, but the inheritor of Sir William's estate will no doubt still be interested in the valuation."

"The contents of the will of Sir William, is it yet known?" asked Chef Maurice, who was on his hands and knees, peering under a rack of half-bottles.

"I believe the execution of the will is being undertaken by Sir William's solicitors, the firm Cranshaw, Cranshaw & Handle in Cowton," said Gilles. "No doubt they will soon be in contact with those whom it concerns."

"Did Sir William ever mention to you who he was bequeathing the estate to?" asked Arthur.

"Sir William was a very private man in those respects, sir."

"He has much family still?" asked Chef Maurice, his voice echoing as he stuck his head into an empty wine barrel which had been serving as decoration and, given the cat hairs, a playhouse for Waffles.

"I believe there is only his nephew, Lady Margaret's son, and of course Lady Margaret, though both are related by marriage only. The young Mr Burton-Trent being her son from her first marriage, you see."

There was something in the way Gilles spoke . . .

"But you don't think he'll inherit, do you?" said Arthur.

Gilles paused. "I don't believe Sir William had seen Mr Timothy Burton-Trent for many years, ever since the gentleman emigrated to the Americas as a young man of twenty."

"Bit of a wild one, eh?" said Arthur.

"One expects his character will have matured over the years," was Gilles's diplomatic reply.

"And Lady Margaret? She is his sister-in-law, after all."

"We shall know in due course, I am sure."

Arthur wandered over to Chef Maurice, who was now standing arms folded, contemplating the dusty silver candleholder screwed high into one wall.

"Found what you were looking for?"

Chef Maurice shook his head. Still frowning, he reached up and tugged at the candleholder, which came away from the wall in his hand.

There was a flurry of fine dust and an unimpressed cough behind them from Gilles, but no further result.

Chef Maurice handed the candleholder to Arthur—who examined it, then handed it on to Gilles—then continued his walk around the cellar, now staring at the ceiling.

Arthur had known Chef Maurice for enough years now to know that whatever the chef did, he did for a reason. It might not always be a well-thought-out, sensible, or even vaguely coherent reason, but at least there always was one. And the explanation for his friend's rather strange behaviour thus far was slowly dawning on Arthur.

"You're looking for a secret passageway, aren't you?" he hissed. He knew he sounded ridiculous, but one often did when one hung around Chef Maurice for any length of time.

His friend beamed at him. "Very good, *mon ami*! If Sir William still had the key, then it is most likely that it was *he* who locked the door after Monsieur Paloni, not the murderer. And so, I conclude that the murderer must have entered from another way. Now if you will help me lift this crate—"

"Maurice, you really have got to stop watching all those detective shows. Not every old house is riddled with hidden passageways leading up to some cunning sliding stone behind the gardener's shed and all that. And even if there was one, don't you think the police might have found it when they searched the place yesterday?"

"Pah, it would be too hard for the police to find," said Chef Maurice, as if this was obvious. "That is why it is secret, *n'est-ce pas*? Aha, you see this?"

He pointed to a high shelf, on which rested yet another row of bottles. The one at the end, though, looked remarkably free from dust. Chef Maurice tugged it down off the shelf.

Mysterious springs declined to ping, no concealed mechanisms whirred into life, and a secret entrance behind the wine racks completely failed to swing open.

"Hmph," said Chef Maurice, and replaced the bottle.

"You know," said Arthur, "there is a simple solution to all this."

"*Oui?*"

"A third key."

Chef Maurice gave this idea due consideration, then shook his head. "*Non*, I think not."

"Why not?" demanded Arthur. "It's a perfectly reasonable explanation. Far more reasonable than anything you've come up with so far."

"Sir William once said to me, he had kept his pair of leather gloves for more than thirty years. He showed them to me, a very fine pair, I recall. A man who does not lose his gloves after thirty years, *mon ami*, is not a man who makes more than one spare key."

There was a mewing sound at their feet, and Arthur looked down into the big, pleading eyes of Waffles, who was staring at the kipper sandwich tucked into Chef Maurice's jacket.

"Ah, *bonjour, petit chat*. You wish for more of Madame Bates' excellent kipper?" Chef Maurice placed the sandwich on the flagstones, and continued on with his search.

"Haven't you had enough kippers for the day?" said Arthur sternly to the cat. "And how did you get down—" He stopped, and stared back up at the stairs. He was almost certain they had closed the—

"Maurice!" He turned around, looking for the chef. "The cat, how did it—"

But Chef Maurice had disappeared.

CHAPTER 10

"So when's your next date with that hunky chef of yours?" PC Sara spun her chair around to face PC Lucy's desk.

"Next Tuesday. And he's not 'my' chef—"

"—*hunky* chef, don't forget that part —"

"—thank you very much. It's still early days, remember?"

"Well, I'd get things wrapped up if I were you. A man who can cook and likes washing up? Snap him up quick, I say."

"I never said he *likes* washing up. It just bothers him to see it all piled up."

PC Lucy sorely wished she'd never told Sara about that particular event. It had been after the naked-photography debacle, when she'd invited Patrick up for a highly apologetic coffee. She'd popped to the bathroom, and next thing she knew he had filled the kitchen sink with hot, soapy water and was getting through the embarrassingly large stack of plates and pans that had been colonising her counter for over a week.

In truth, he'd looked rather attractive in her yellow washing-up gloves, but she wasn't about to tell PC Sara that.

"So when do I get to meet this domestic god?"

"Uh-uh, no way. Not anytime soon. You'll give him the third degree, I know you will."

"Shame. Especially as I've just been on that Advanced Interview and Interrogation Techniques course." PC Sara held up a ring binder.

"Exactly. Anyway, one step at a time."

PC Sara tilted her head. "Ah. So I take it you haven't told him yet about . . . "

"No! And thank you for bringing *that* up again."

"You're welcome. I just think it's ridiculous for you to pretend—"

"Look, I'll tell him eventually. We're still in the dating stage, it's not like he's my official boyfriend."

PC Sara grinned. "'Yet', you mean?"

"I'm still deciding," said PC Lucy, with as much aloofness as she could muster.

"Sure." PC Sara rolled her eyes. "Well, you better get on with it, or I might have to pop over to Beakley for lunch to take my own look. How about the other chefs? Any potential there I should know about?"

PC Lucy thought about Alf and Chef Maurice. Her mind rebelled as she tried to picture either of them on a date.

"Not your type," she said firmly.

"Pity."

Across the room, the main phone line started to ring. PC Alistair sprawled himself over his desk in an effort to get to the receiver.

"Cowton and Beakley Constabulary . . . Yes, she does, why? . . . You might be better phoning the fire brigade if . . . Sorry, what? . . . Just a moment . . . "

He put his hand over the mouthpiece. "Um, PC Gavistone, I think you'd better get this one . . . "

PC Lucy walked over and took the phone off Alistair. "Hello, Gavistone speaking."

She listened carefully to Arthur's convoluted babbling. Eventually, she thought she had the gist of things. But—

"Hang on, slow down, Mr Wordington-Smythe. Say that again. He's got himself stuck *where?*"

One of the important considerations in the design of a secret passageway is that it should take up as little space as possible. Some people, especially the meticulous type who own their own retractable tape measures, get suspicious when they find that their house is significantly smaller on the inside than out. Thus, over the ages, cunning architects have learnt to sequester little pockets of space into the floor plans where no one is likely to notice.

The more complicated and rambling the building, the easier this is—which probably explains why one does not often find hidden passages in your typical two-bedroom terraced maisonette.

119

The construction of this particular passageway, which appeared to date back at least a few hundred years from the look of the stonework, had been commissioned by some previous owner of Bourne Hall, who—to get to the pinch point of the problem, as it were—had clearly been a gentleman of somewhat slimline stature.

Halfway up the winding, dusty steps, the staircase narrowed to make room for the rear portion of a chimney stack or some other type of recess. It was at this point in his explorations that Chef Maurice had come to an abrupt halt.

"Turning sideways would have worked for most people," said Arthur, as he led PC Lucy down the cellar stairs. "To be fair to him, the stonework isn't exactly helping. It's too rough, too much friction to just slide on through."

"Can't he just come back down the way he went?" asked PC Lucy.

"We tried that. But he seems to have got himself completely wedged in." Arthur led her over to a stack of wooden wine crates in the corner. On closer inspection, she noticed they had been nailed together and placed atop a set of small castors, allowing the whole construction to be wheeled aside to reveal the archway through which Chef Maurice had disappeared.

PC Lucy rubbed her eyes and stared at the rows and rows of bottles surrounding them. Just being down here was giving her a hangover from passive alcohol proximity. Either that, or it was the singing. If you could call it singing.

"Why is he . . . doing that?" asked PC Lucy, as Chef Maurice launched into yet another verse of 'La Marseillaise'.

"Gilles is upstairs, looking for the other end of the passageway. We know Waffles must have got in that way. It's now just a matter of finding it."

"I see."

"—*sous nos drapeaux que la victoire*—"

"I do feel our own national anthem rather short-changes us on the rousing lyrics," commented Arthur. "At least the French one has some *ooomph*."

PC Lucy gave the air a sniff. "Is it me, or does this cellar smell of kippers?"

Arthur explained Chef Maurice's kipper-cat-secret-passageway idea.

"Impressive," she said at last. "If you knew the cat would try to get down here, you just had to watch for where she appeared. Completely barmy, of course, but effective, I'll give him that."

She gave the fake pile of wine cases a little push. She could see now that the whole contraption wasn't quite as tall as the archway, leaving a cat-sized gap at the top through which Waffles had squeezed.

"Did Gilles know about this hidden staircase?"

"He claims not to."

"Really? Hmmm."

"—*ton triomphe et notre gloire*— Ah, Monsieur Gilles! You have had success!"

Gilles's voice echoed down the stairway. "Apparently so, sir. Thanks to sir's extremely vocal efforts, I located the other end of this passageway behind the bookcase upstairs, next to Sir William's bedroom. This does rather neatly solve the question of the occasional empty half-bottle I would find by his bedside in the morning. Now, if sir would take the end of this rope . . . Mr Wordington-Smythe, can you hear me?"

"Loud and clear."

"If you could assist by applying an upwards force on, ahem, Mr Manchot from your end, and I will pull on the rope from up here. Together, I trust our efforts will free him."

Arthur looked at PC Lucy, who gave him a 'I'm not paid enough to do this' shrug. He sighed and disappeared up the stairs.

"All right, Gilles, I'm here. Ready when you are."

"Very good, sir. On the count of three . . . "

There was a thump, a yell, and a certain amount of French swearing.

"Is everything okay?" called PC Lucy.

Arthur came back down the stairs, brushing dust off his sleeves. "All present and correct."

"Ah, is that Mademoiselle Lucy I hear?" Chef Maurice's voice floated down the stairwell. "I must tell her about my—"

"Oh no, you don't! Don't you dare try coming back down this way!" yelled Arthur. "I'm not getting you unstuck again. We'll come up the other way and meet you on the landing."

A few minutes later, the little group congregated in the corridor outside Sir William's bedroom. Chef Maurice was covered in dust and a few cobwebs, but otherwise no worse for wear. At his feet, Waffles circled and purred, on the off chance there was another kipper sandwich to be had.

The bookcase had been slid aside to reveal a narrow archway, similar to the one down in the cellar. From the castor marks on the floorboards, PC Lucy could see that the bookcase did not sit quite flush with the wall, allowing yet another Waffles-sized gap behind. So this was how the cat had got in.

As well as the murderer.

"There's been quite a bit of traffic," said PC Lucy, shining her torch down into the dusty entrance. "Impossible to make out any individual footprints, though."

Gilles was regarding the hidden staircase with pursed lips, though whether this was due to its existence or the lack of cleaning was hard to tell.

"We had the upstairs carpets relaid last year. The fitter was insistent that the measurements did not add up, but in the end it was all laid perfectly. This certainly explains *that* little mystery."

"And the mystery of how the murderer got out of a locked cellar," said Arthur. "Sir William must have locked the door after Paloni left him. Rather scuppered our perpetrator's plans, that. We'd have never thought to look for another way in otherwise."

"We?" Chef Maurice looked indignant.

"You honestly didn't know anything about this passage-way?" said PC Lucy to Gilles, trying to keep the scepticism out of her voice.

"I assure you, madam, I hadn't the slightest inkling. If I had, I would have insisted most strongly that Sir William brick it up for security reasons. It quite invalidates our insurance policy, I'm sure."

PC Lucy glanced around the corridor at the row of closed guest room doors. Any of the visitors could have slipped out that evening and hurried down these steps . . .

"Well, clearly, someone else knew about its existence."

"So it seems," said Gilles. He looked a trifle ill.

"Which of last night's guests would be most familiar with the layout of Bourne Hall?"

"Lady Margaret has been visiting the Hall for decades, of course. Mr Lafoute too," said Gilles, with some re-luctance. "Mr Resnick has stayed with us several times in the past few years, and Mrs Lafoute, though she has not been a frequent visitor thus far, did spend a fortnight at the Hall soon after her marriage to Mr Lafoute."

"So, all of the guests, except for Monsieur Paloni, had been often enough a visitor to have the potential for knowledge of this staircase?" said Chef Maurice.

"Looks like it," said PC Lucy, notepad out.

"Hallo, what's this?" said Arthur, bending over Waffles, who was pawing at something just inside the archway. It was a white handkerchief, now grey with dust.

"It must be from the murderer!" Chef Maurice grabbed the handkerchief. "Perhaps we can trace the *parfum* or cologne—" He stuck the cloth to his nose, inhaled deeply, then exploded into a fit of sneezes.

"Wait!" PC Lucy grabbed the handkerchief before Chef Maurice could blow his nose on a key piece of evidence. Arthur, sighing, proffered his own blue-checked handkerchief to his friend.

She turned the handkerchief over in her hands. It was made of stiff cotton, of very good quality. In one corner, embroidered in light grey thread, was an initial.

A curly letter 'A'

CHAPTER 11

The next morning, Arthur and Chef Maurice caught the 7.34 a.m. train from Beakley, changing at Oxford, to London Paddington. Arthur found himself a seat wedged in amongst the morning commuters, who drooped over their newspapers like rows of thirsty sunflowers. To his left, a young man in a navy blue suit was dozing with his head against the window; to his right, a middle-aged woman in purple tweed was ferociously consuming the day's financial pages, throwing the occasional scathing look at the large picnic hamper on Arthur's lap.

He tried to avoid her gaze and buried his nose in the recently released autobiography of Keith Savage, often dubbed 'the angriest chef in Britain'. This was his second book to date, titled *Seared, Scarred and Savaged: Tales from the World's Best, Greatest and Most Awesome Kitchen*.

(The editor who'd tentatively suggested to Savage that the book's subtitle wasn't entirely accurate, and possibly open to litigious challenge, was later found hiding on the ledge outside his office window, and had to be coaxed back down under the promise of never having to work with celebrity chefs again. He was also given carte blanche to commission a series of books on cupcakes.)

"*Excusez-moi, excusez-moi,* ooops, *pardon, madame* . . . "

Arthur watched Chef Maurice squeeze and elbow his way back down the carriage, accompanied by a series of yelps and discontented muttering.

"Any luck finding the sandwich trolley?"

"*Non,* but I did see Mademoiselle Lucy with one of her *collègues.* But do not worry, I make sure that they did not see me."

Arthur looked up at his friend's large pork-pie hat (which he liked to wear on days out), giant moustache and big heavy winter coat.

"We can but hope."

"But to be sure we reach Madame Ariane before they do, perhaps we should command a taxi to her hotel?"

"Not a bad idea."

PC Lucy had expressly forbidden them to engage in any amateur investigations of their own. Which, as Chef Maurice had pointed out, meant they'd simply have to get on with their investigating in a more covert manner.

The lid of the picnic hamper swung up, and a little pink snout poked out.

The woman on Arthur's right gave a shriek. "What *is* that?"

"He is a micro-pig, *madame,*" said Chef Maurice, extracting a handful of sow nuts from his pocket and offering them to the snout, which snuffled them up greedily. "His name is Hamilton."

"I . . . I refuse to sit here next to someone carrying *livestock*!" The woman struggled to her feet and pushed her way down the aisle.

Chef Maurice sat down in the newly vacated seat and made himself comfortable. Hamilton had now fully pushed back the hamper lid, and was staring around the train carriage with great interest.

"Are you sure we should have brought Hamilton with us?" said Arthur, handing the picnic hamper over to Chef Maurice and jiggling his leaden legs. Hamilton might be a micro-pig, but he had definitely put on weight since Chef Maurice had adopted him a few months ago.

"They say it is important for animals to have a variety of stimulation," said Chef Maurice firmly.

Hamilton, for his part, having ascertained that none of the dozy humans around him were going to give him any more sow nuts, ducked back inside the hamper to carry on with his morning nap.

In her suite at The Belvedere, Piccadilly, Ariane Lafoute greeted them with perfumed kisses and led them over to the low seats by the windows. She did not seem overly concerned by the presence of her tiny third guest, and even poured some Evian into a bowl for Hamilton to lap up.

It was a crisp December day outside, and from their vantage point, they could look down and watch the tiny muffled-up passers-by hurry along Lower Regent Street.

"A coffee?" said Ariane, waving her hand at the silver coffee pot. She was wearing a tight black turtleneck, a discreet string of pearls, and well-cut grey tailored trousers.

"With three sugars, *merci*. You have recovered, *madame*, from the terrible events of the last Saturday?"

Ariane gave a little shrug, as if to suggest that the murder of one's host happened all the time back where she came from. "Bertie is most upset, of course. He and Sir William were very close. But for me, I cannot say I knew him well."

This was a stark change from the trembling young woman they had last encountered a few days before. Ariane appeared to have regained full control of her icy poise, and the tilt of her head discouraged further enquiries into her well-being.

The coffee table was strewn with papers, including the architectural plans they had seen in the Lafoutes' room at Bourne Hall.

"May I?" said Arthur, indicating the building drawings. Ariane nodded vaguely, then resumed staring out of the window, chin rested on delicate wrist.

Chef Maurice wiggled a detailed sketch of a wine label out of the pile. The label read: *La Fleur de Lafoute*.

"Ah, you plan, *madame*, to make a second wine?"

Ariane gave him a curt nod. "It is time. All the best chateaux make not just one, but two or even three wines. My *grand-mère*, she has insisted for a long time that all our grapes go into the one wine, Chateau Lafoute. But with modern techniques, our winemaking can now be done with much greater precision. Especially"—she shifted the papers to show a detailed cross-section of the new proposed winery building—"if we can install these smaller fermentation tanks, to allow each parcel of land to ferment and mature separately, we will be allowed more control in the final blending. And by separating our production into two wines, we can achieve even greater quality for our first wine."

A change had come over Ariane. There was a sparkle in her eyes and a fiery warmth in her voice that Arthur had not heard before.

Chef Maurice had noticed it too. "I see you are most passionate about your wines, *madame*."

"If I am not, who will be?" replied Ariane, with some vehemence. "My *grand-mère*, she is ninety-two. Soon it will come a time that I must lead the chateau."

"And your husband?"

She waved a hand. "Before we were married, he saw it all as a game, a 'hobby'," she said, deploying the word with distaste. "But now I have made him come to see, it is not play, it is work. Hard work! It is not simply a job. To make good wine, it must consume your life."

Arthur flipped over another sheet. It was a colour sketch of rows and rows of gleaming fermentation tanks and a new maturation room with oak barrels, piled three high, stretching as far as the artist's eye could see.

"Very attractive. I hope the investor meetings are going well?" said Arthur, remembering what Bertie had said about the couple's purpose for being in London.

Ariane's lip curled. "These business people, they have no vision. They want to see a return in two years, five years. But a great wine may not show its beauty for decades. The replanting of vines can take ten, twenty years to be truly ready. They are too impatient. They have no understanding."

"And Sir William?" asked Chef Maurice. "Did he offer his support?"

Ariane looked up sharply. "For a long time, I have asked my husband to speak with him. Sir William has been an admirer of the château for years. I was sure that he would have . . . " Her voice trailed off. "But my husband, he would act strange, very proud in this matter. He refused to even approach him with the subject."

Arthur thought about the note they'd found in Sir William's pocket. Perhaps it was at this point that Ariane had decided to explore other modes of persuasion.

"But it does not matter now," finished Ariane with another wave of her hand.

"You have more meetings?" said Chef Maurice.

Ariane paused, then nodded, slightly uncertain. "There are a few . . . that I have hopes for."

There was the distant *ping* of the lift in the hallway, and familiar voices could be heard approaching the suite's double doors.

"—seen a hotel like this, miss. Look, they even have sweets left out on the little tables, that's fancy—"

"Alistair, this is a police investigation, not Disneyland."

131

"Yes, miss. But do you think we might have time to see *Les Misérables* afterwards—"

"Shhh! Now if you could *try* acting like a police officer, and not like a kid on a school trip . . . "

There was an official-sounding rat-a-tat-tat on the door.

Ariane raised a perfectly shaped eyebrow at Arthur. "Your police, they are like the hunting dogs. They sniff and sniff," she said, uncrossing her legs and drifting over to the door.

"Mrs Lafoute? I'm PC Gavistone, we spoke yesterday afternoon on the phone? I hope I'm not disturbing you—" PC Lucy stopped as she noticed Arthur and Chef Maurice sitting there with coffee cups in their hands.

"No, not at all, please join us," said Ariane.

PC Lucy took a seat at the end of the sofa, while PC Alistair sat down on the footrest, gazing around the suite with wide-eyed amazement. Hamilton, knowing a soft touch when he saw one, head-butted the freckled young man on the ankle and gave a pointed look at the pile of apples in the carved fruit bowl.

"I won't keep you long, Mrs Lafoute, seeing as you have guests," said PC Lucy, glaring at Chef Maurice and Arthur.

"By all means, please," said Ariane. "Your work is important, and the sooner you have discovered who could have committed such a grave crime . . . "

There was a wet crunch-crunch-crunch sound from under the table. PC Alistair looked up guiltily, an apple core in his hand.

"This may sound odd," said PC Lucy, with another glare at Chef Maurice, "but what do you know about a concealed passageway between the wine cellar and the upper floor of Bourne Hall?"

"Passageway?" Ariane looked confused. "I had not heard of such a thing."

"The entrance was hidden behind the bookcase, the one on the landing between Sir William's bedroom and the guest rooms."

"The English, they are so strange," said Ariane, with a little sigh. "To have a cellar and install such security, then to have a secret entrance hidden behind some books? It is madness."

"So you didn't know anything about it?"

"Not at all. But why do you a—" Ariane stopped. The implication of a secret way down to the cellars, the scene of the horrific crime, had clearly just sunk in. She looked, thought Arthur, suddenly scared.

"You think that is how . . . " she started.

PC Lucy pulled a clear plastic bag out of her jacket. It was the white handkerchief from yesterday. "Do you recognise this?" she said, placing the bag on the table. "It was found in the entrance to the passageway."

Ariane stared at it, mesmerised, her hand stretched out to pick it up. For a moment, an odd expression—confusion? anger?—flitted across her face, then she nodded slowly.

"I cannot be sure, but this appears to belong to my husband," she said.

"But why then is there the 'A'?" said Chef Maurice, before PC Lucy could jump in.

"For Albert, of course. You did not think his parents would have named him Bertie?" Ariane sniffed. "I much prefer to call him Albert, too. Bertie, it is a silly name."

PC Lucy carefully picked up the bag. "Is Mr Lafoute also here at the hotel?"

"No. He left early this morning. He is probably at his club, The Hansdowne. On Graham Street."

PC Lucy made a note of this. "Thank you for your time, Mrs Lafoute. We'll be in touch if there are any more questions. In the meantime, if you have anything you'd like to discuss with us"—such as why your husband's handkerchief was found near the scene of the crime, was the unspoken message—"do give us a call."

After the two police officers had departed, Ariane collapsed back down on the couch. She looked suddenly weary, as if the last five minutes' conversation had drained a decade from her.

"Should we give Bertie a call?" said Arthur, determined to play the concerned acquaintance. "Give him a heads-up, so to speak?"

Ariane shook her head. "They do not pass on messages from outside at his club. And they forbid them to use their phones. I think that is why the men go there," she added, with a wan smile.

"Did Monsieur Bertie ever speak of any secret passageways in Bourne Hall?" said Chef Maurice.

"No, certainly not."

"What about that night at Bourne Hall," said Arthur, "when you were upstairs? Did you hear anything unusual? Notice anything out of the ordinary?"

"Someone slipping from behind a bookcase, you mean?" said Ariane, raising an eyebrow. "No. I remember hearing noises, the banging, from downstairs. I heard someone, I think it must have been Chuck, running past outside. Bertie, he went first to see what the noise was. I stayed a moment, I was . . . tired, then when the noise did not stop, I followed."

"Did you see anyone else in the corridor upstairs?"

"Only Charles. He was just coming from his room. He asked me what was happening, but I said I did not know. So we came downstairs."

There was a thump from under the table, and Hamilton stuck his snout out to see if he had caused sufficient disruption to the fruit bowl. Chef Maurice waggled a finger at the little pig.

"You will spoil your appetite," he told Hamilton. He looked back up at Ariane. "When you were at Bourne Hall, Sir William wished to speak to you in private, *n'est-ce pas*? Was that usual?"

"No. As I said, I hardly knew him."

"May I ask what you spoke about?"

"He asked me many questions about Chateau Lafoute. The history, the changes my great-grandfather made, the stocks we have still of the older vintages, how the chateau operated during the wars. I told him he should speak to my *grand-mère*, not me."

"Any reason he'd have suddenly been so interested in the chateau's history?" said Arthur, who harboured doubts as to how much of Ariane's story was true. Despite his limited personal experience of such matters, he was pretty sure that clandestine lovers did not usually meet up merely to discuss the historical details of Bordeaux chateaux.

Ariane shrugged. "I assumed he wanted to make an introduction of our wines for the night's tasting. I thought also perhaps Bertie had discussed with him the new winery plans, but he says later he did not."

After a few more polite enquiries regarding the future winery, Arthur and Chef Maurice took their leave—though first they had to locate Hamilton, who had managed to trap himself in the bedroom wardrobe.

"A most clever *cochon*," said Chef Maurice, patting the hamper's lid as they stood in the lift.

Arthur raised a questioning eyebrow.

"You did not see, *mon ami*? While we were in the bedroom, I had the chance to look at Monsieur Bertie's clothing. Madame Ariane was not lying. I found many such handkerchiefs as the one that we found at Bourne Hall."

"She didn't look too happy telling that to the police. I suppose she knew they'd find out anyway, best to come clean at the start. It's not exactly binding evidence, after all."

"But it shows that Monsieur Bertie is definitely in knowledge of the passageway."

"So it seems. A cool customer that one, I mean, Ariane. Hard to believe that she and Sir William were . . . you know . . . "

Chef Maurice looked at his friend curiously. "You still believe there was *une liaison* between them?"

"You don't?"

Chef Maurice shook his head. "Madame Ariane, she is like the wines her family makes in Bordeaux. They are stern, powerful, strong beneath the silk, as you say. But Sir William, his preferred wines were the wines of *Bourgogne*. *Fragile*, subtle, wines of quiet beauty."

"So you're telling me that just because Sir William preferred his Burgundy to his Bordeaux, he couldn't possibly have been having an affair with Ariane Lafoute?"

"*Exactement!*"

"So how do you explain the note?"

"Ah." Chef Maurice rubbed his moustache. "That, I have not yet discovered."

The lift pinged, and they exited into the lobby. "So where do we go next? Fancy tackling our Mr Lafoute?"

Chef Maurice nodded. "But first we must stop at Mulling Street. I have something important I must collect."

The door of Mingleberry & Judd, fine wine merchants of Mayfair, gave a polite tinkle, and the silence of hundreds of bottles of wine maturing slowly on the shelves was broken by the sound of two voices raised in argument.

"—get over to The Hansdowne as quickly as possible, else Lucy and Alistair will have already cornered Bertie—"

"Bah, you must have patience, *mon ami*. I tell you there is no need for rush, this will be just a small moment—"

"You, in a wine shop? This I'd like to see."

"Then you will. Ah, *bonjour*, Monsieur Mingleberry."

Mr Mingleberry adjusted his tie and hurried across the room to welcome his visitors.

"Mr Manchot, how good to see you. I assume you're here to check upon your Christmas order? We were just about to start the packing and labelling today. Always good to miss the postal rush. I'm rather taken with the wrapping paper Mr Judd ordered this year. Midnight blue, thick weave, it'll look quite fetching under the tree."

"*Très jolie*," said Chef Maurice, casting a glance at the neatly wrapped parcels along the counter. "But today, I come simply to buy a book about wine. Come, Arthur, you are a writer, tell me which to buy."

As well as supplying fine wines to London's oenophile population, Mingleberry & Judd also stocked the city's most comprehensive collection of guides, histories, dissertations and tasting bibles concerning the humble wine grape. Whether you were in search of a scientific discussion of the various Burgundian grape clones, a travel guide to Santa Monica's vineyards, or a book of vinous quotations for your after-dinner speeches, this was the place to go.

"What kind of book are you looking for?" said Arthur suspiciously. His friend was not known for his love of the written word, unless you counted the pile of old Encyclopaedia Britannicas he used to weigh down terrines in the walk-in.

"I wish to find a book of the famous wines of the world. It is for Alf. It is important for him to recognise and appreciate the history of our great wines."

"And to stop him turning them into mulled wine?"

"That, also."

"What about this one?" Arthur reached up and pulled out a thick tome titled *The World's Hundred Greatest Wines*. "Look, they even have pictures of all the labels, and maps of the regions."

"Would you gentlemen be interested in trying the '83 vintage Port from Loffburns?" Mr Mingleberry appeared behind them, holding a silver tray with three small glasses of dark red liquid. "Just coming up to its peak, in my opinion. Quite outstanding."

Chef Maurice downed his sample, then offered the empty glass to Hamilton in his hamper for a sniff. The little pig sneezed.

"I will take one bottle," he announced.

"Two for me," said Arthur, who was definitely partial to a good glass of Port by the fireside.

Mr Mingleberry nodded in satisfaction, and reappeared just moments later with three neatly wrapped bottles. "Unless you would like us to send them with the rest of your order?"

"That will not be necessary." Chef Maurice took the bottles and added them to Hamilton's hamper.

"You sure that's a good idea?" said Arthur, looking at the little pig, who was now sniffing at the wrapping.

"They will be safe. He does not enjoy the Port."

"Just as well, he's probably underage."

"A little Calvados in his water, though . . . "

Mr Mingleberry was fiddling with his tiepin. "I suppose," he said, after a moment, "you have heard the terrible news about Sir William?"

They nodded.

"Did you know him well?" asked Arthur.

"He was one of our oldest and dearest clients," said Mr Mingleberry, now wringing his hands. "We always managed to secure him the allocations he desired, and he was always constant in his support of us. A loyal client, and most generous, too. He took our whole team out to lunch after we managed to secure him three cases of the '96 Latour *en primeur*."

"Had you seen him much lately?"

"I'm afraid not. He had been coming to London less and less, and when he did, it was usually to attend the auctions. He was purchasing more and more at auction too," sniffed Mr Mingleberry, like a wife alluding to a barely tolerated mistress, "but I suppose one cannot blame him. The old and rare wine market has been seeing a startling ascent in these last few years." He shook his head. "I do hope whoever comes into inheritance of Sir William's collection will take great care over it . . . "

They left Mr Mingleberry to his Christmas wrapping and headed down the street, Chef Maurice carrying hamper in one hand and book in the other, and Arthur carrying doubts as to how enthusiastic Meryl would be to discover yet another addition to his Port collection.

"Do not fear, *mon ami*," said Chef Maurice, reading his friend's expression. "You may keep your bottles in our cellar. Madame Meryl will never need to see them."

Like Sir William, Arthur maintained a small collection of bottles down in the cellars of Le Cochon Rouge, purportedly because of its superior temperature and humidity stability compared to his own at home, but in actuality to keep Meryl from knowing the exact tally of bottles he'd accumulated over the years.

(On her part, Meryl had no such qualms about her own shoe collection, in the happy knowledge that her husband was entirely incapable of telling one pair from another, and was happy to accept each new incoming shoebox as 'a real bargain, darling'.)

It was a short walk over to The Hansdowne Club, which stood on a quiet back street off Berkeley Square.

Outside, they found PC Lucy pacing up and down, while PC Alistair studied a leaflet of the evening's theatre showings.

"What is the matter?" said Chef Maurice.

PC Lucy spun to face them, pointing an accusatory finger at the bowler-hatted doorman. "Of all the stupid, outmoded, sexist, pig-headed—"

"They don't let ladies in," explained PC Alistair. He held up the leaflet to Arthur. "Do you think I should see *Phantom* or *Cats* first?"

"Can you not ask Monsieur Bertie to come outside?" asked Chef Maurice.

"*You* ask him." PC Lucy shot a hostile look at the doorman, who tipped his hat politely.

"I'm afraid, sir, that club rules do not allow us to pass on messages from ladies to our members when they are resident at the club." He coughed. "The rule was instituted after the Wife Riots of April 1903."

"I can just imagine," said Arthur, rather glumly.

"What about us?" said Chef Maurice. "May we go inside to visit Monsieur Bertie?"

"I will enquire within, sir." The doorman opened the door a crack and spoke in hushed tones to someone standing inside. "Please tell Mr Lafoute that there is a . . . "

"Mr Wordington-Smythe, Mr Manchot, and . . . " Arthur looked at PC Alistair.

"Bobbin, sir."

" . . . Mr Bobbin to see him."

"And a Monsieur Hamilton, too," said Chef Maurice, lifting the hamper lid to reveal the dozing pig. "He is a gentleman pig, of course."

PC Lucy made a choking sound.

A few minutes later, the door opened wider and a tailcoated attendant appeared.

"Mr Lafoute will see you gentlemen in the Billiards Room," he said with a small bow. "But no pets, I'm afraid, sir."

"Eh? But what must I do with—"

"No pets, sir."

Chef Maurice threw a beseeching look at PC Lucy. Hamilton, now awake, stuck his head out of his hamper and trained his most pathetic 'take me home' look on the policewoman.

"Oh, fine!" Cheeks flushed, she grabbed the hamper and shoved the clear plastic bag containing Bertie's handkerchief at PC Alistair. "Get confirmation that this belongs to Mr Lafoute. I'll see if I can track down Mr Paloni and Mr Resnick while I'm here. If they're not hiding out in some men's-only club too." She stalked off down the street, hamper in hand, leaving the three males standing in embarrassed silence.

Arthur, as a right-thinking fellow of the modern world, was of course in full support of PC Lucy's outrage at this archaic, woefully discriminatory system. That said, as they passed various handsome rooms, with freshly pressed newspapers laid out and various club members snoozing peacefully with copies of the *England Observer* rising and falling gently on their bellies, he experienced the sudden inexplicable urge to join them.

He shook his head. "Got to move with the times, I guess. Not right, keeping women out in this day and age."

Chef Maurice snorted. "Bah, the Beakley Ladies' Institute refused for me to join! Is that not also unfair?"

"Well, yes, but I know for a fact that that had nothing to do with you not being a woman, Maurice. Mr Evans is a member, and Meryl says everyone raves about his raspberry shortcake. They didn't let you join because you called the chairwoman 'a lady with the face of a horse and a *derrière* to match'."

"She dared to disqualify my *tarte aux pommes*!"

"It was an amateur baking contest, Maurice. Which means chefs can't enter."

"Then how will people know that my *tarte* is the best?"

Thankfully, their conversation was halted by their arrival at the door of a low-ceilinged room dominated by a giant billiard table. Large leather-bound journals lined the walls, and comfortable dark green leather armchairs were dotted around the edge of the room. One of these armchairs was currently home to Bertie Lafoute, who was staring down at a sheet of typed paper with the glazed look of a man whose thoughts are very far away indeed.

On spotting his visitors, though, he jumped up like an eager schoolboy and shook their hands. "Arthur, Maurice, how spiffing to see you. Sorry I didn't see you there, I've just had a bit of a shock," he added, stuffing the piece of paper into his pocket.

"Not a bad one, I hope?" said Arthur.

"No, no. Not at all." Bertie appeared to notice Alistair for the first time. "And PC Bobbin, too. That's right, isn't it? Are you on your day off?"

Alistair, who was wearing his usual police uniform, looked at Arthur for guidance.

"Alistair is thinking of catching *The Phantom of the Opera* this evening," said Arthur. "Though he appears to have forgotten to bring his pitchfork."

"Splendid musical, and a fantastic set, of course." Bertie started humming happily, then seemed to remember himself. "Sorry. I suppose at a time like this . . . " His face sobered up.

They settled down, and a waiter materialised to take their tea and coffee orders.

"So what brings you to London?" said Bertie.

Chef Maurice leaned back in his chair and clasped his hands over his stomach. "We have come," he said, eying Bertie carefully, "to speak to you of secret passageways."

Bertie froze. "Secret passageways, you say?"

Chef Maurice outlined yesterday's discovery at Bourne Hall, though he omitted the finding of the handkerchief.

"You spent much time as a child at Bourne Hall, *n'est-ce pas*? And as a *jeune homme*, returning from the school holidays. Perhaps you are familiar with this hidden way?"

Bertie's eyes widened, then he started to shake his head vigorously. "No, no, not at all! In fact, I'd all but—"

He stopped.

"All but what, *monsieur*?"

Bertie remained silent, his gaze darting back and forth between them.

"You had, perhaps, forgotten the existence of the passageway, until very recently?"

A jerky nod. "Until you just mentioned it. I swear, it never crossed my mind! It sounds daft, but my memory's always been a bit funny, and we all thought the attacker had come in from outside—"

"So you *were* aware of the passageway, on the night of Sir William's murder?"

"N-no! Not at all! I mean, I must have known about it, deep down, of course, but like I said, the idea that—" He stopped, and looked around at his three visitors. "Anyway, why does any of this matter? I told the police already, I was with Ariane the whole time when we were upstairs that night. I never went anywhere. She'll tell you!"

"We have spoken already with Madame Ariane. She too says she has no knowledge of any secret passageway."

"You spoke with my wife?" Bertie sat up straighter, managing to emit a certain degree of quavery indignation.

"A simple visit. There is no law about that, *non*?" said Chef Maurice. "And we also come to speak to you about a handkerchief." He motioned to Alistair, who held up the plastic bag. "This was found in the kitchens of Bourne Hall."

"Ac—" began Arthur, but Chef Maurice's steel-capped boot was quick to deliver a warning message through Arthur's ankle bone to his tongue.

"Oh yes, that's one of mine," said Bertie, still shaken, but relieved to be moving on to more manageable topics. "I'm always losing them. Ariane complains we have to order a new dozen every few months." The mention of

Ariane seemed to trigger another bout of jitters. "If you'll excuse me, gentlemen, I must be getting back to the hotel. Ariane is expecting me. Do feel free to stay for lunch—I'll let the front desk know. I'm sure they'll be able to find you a table."

With that, Bertie stood up stiffly, shook their hands, then hared out of the room.

"Well, that was odd," said Arthur, in the silence that ensued.

"Do you think I should have arrested him?" asked PC Alistair.

"Not enough to go on," said Arthur, with the confidence of a man known to enjoy the occasional crime novel. "Knowing-but-sort-of-not-knowing about a secret passageway isn't exactly a crime."

Chef Maurice nodded, staring at Bertie's empty chair. "You saw, *mon ami*, how quick he was to say he was not alone when upstairs that night?"

"Indeed. So what do we do now?"

"It is obvious," said Chef Maurice, pulling out his battered watch.

"It is?"

"Of course. As Monsieur Bertie reminds us, it is now the time for lunch."

The dining room of The Hansdowne Club was full of well-heeled and well-padded gentlemen of a certain age, enjoying their lunches in peaceful solitude, with their folded newspapers mounted on special silver stands to allow the cutting and chewing of food without interruption to their perusal of the day's news. A few were sat together in small groups, though this did not cause any discernible difference in their mode of silent eating.

PC Alistair sat staring around the room, agog at his surroundings. "Does everyone in London belong to one of these club things?" he asked, picking up a monogrammed fork.

"Hardly," said Arthur, settling back into his chair and picking up the wine list. "You usually have to be recommended by at least two other members, and the fees are astronomical."

"Hmph," said Chef Maurice, returning from an investigation of the cheese trolley. "Far too many blues, not a single goat's cheese. And the brie, it is not ripe at all!"

"Criminal, indeed. Though I have to say I'm rather impressed by the wine list. Excellent selection, even the half-bottles, and the prices are extremely fair."

"I'm so glad to hear you say so, Arthur," said a silken voice from behind them. Without turning around, Arthur's gaze fell to the bottom of the wine menu.

Hand-selected with care by our cellar consultant Charles Resnick, M.W.

Blast, thought Arthur, and turned around with an exaggerated expression of pleasant astonishment.

"Charles, what a surprise to see you here!"

"Likewise. I had no idea they let non-members take lunch here," said Resnick.

"Care to join us?" said Arthur, determined to play the bigger man. Plus, Resnick was technically a suspect in the murder case. Alistair surely had all kinds of pressing questions for him.

He shot a glance over at the young policeman, who was staring up at the chandeliered ceiling in undisguised awe.

"Perhaps another time," said Resnick. "I'm just here to discuss the New Year's Eve wine list with Mr Barries, then I'm needed over at Guthries for this week's auction. Quite a charming little line-up. There's a '29 Chateau Chèvre come up in magnum, never seen on the market before. One of my better discoveries, if I do say so. A gentleman of my acquaintance recently bought a Scottish castle —"

As one does, thought Arthur.

"—and they found a fake partition wall in the cellar. You can guess what they found behind. Dozens of bottles in perfect condition, including some extremely interesting pre-war bottlings. You really should come along, pick something up for your cellar." Resnick extracted a glossy brochure from his briefcase and placed it on the table.

"*Merci*, we will try to attend," said Chef Maurice, with one eye on the dessert trolley as it wheeled on by. "But we also have another auction to attend later this afternoon."

"Ah, if that's the case, keep the reins on this one"— Resnick clamped a thin hand to Arthur's shoulder—"we wouldn't want to bankrupt him, ha ha."

"Ha ha," said Arthur.

Resnick nodded at PC Alistair, who was painstakingly counting the array of cutlery before him. "I suppose you've been here to see good old Bertie, then? Following up all 'the leads', as they say? I think you'll find he's a rather lucky young man. I'll be looking forward to doing much business with him in the future."

"You're working with Chateau Lafoute?" Arthur was more than a little surprised. It was common knowledge that Chateau Lafoute preferred to sell direct to their long-standing client base, opting out of the Bordeaux fine wine marketplace completely. Brokers like Resnick usually only got a look in when it came to the secondary market for older vintages.

"The chateau? Hardly. I'm talking about the Bourne Hall collection." He looked at their faces. "Oh, did he not tell you?"

"Tell us what?" demanded Chef Maurice, who did not take well to suspense when he wasn't the one creating it.

"I suppose the solicitors only visited this morning—the poor boy was in quite a state of shock when I came across him earlier. Sir William left everything to Bertie, you see. The Hall, the cellar, all his investments, everything."

"To Bertie?!" said Arthur and Chef Maurice.

Resnick gave a thin-lipped smile. "Yes, it appears you've gained a new neighbour. Now, if you'll excuse me . . . "

"Should I go arrest Mr Bertie now?" asked PC Alistair urgently, as Resnick walked away.

Arthur looked at Chef Maurice. "Rather changes everything, doesn't it?"

Chef Maurice tut-tutted as he examined the slice of cake he'd liberated from the passing dessert trolley. "The English, they still cannot make a good *opéra* cake. The layers, see, they are uneven. And"—he sniffed at a forkful—"there is not enough coffee. But yes," he added, seeing Arthur's expression, "this does very much change the investigation. But to inherit a fortune is not a crime. We must proceed with care."

His gaze fell onto the auction brochure left there by Resnick.

"You know, *mon ami*, I have always had in mind to attend a wine auction . . . "

CHAPTER 12

The main auction room at Guthries was a hive of genteel activity. Chairs were laid out in rows all the way up to the dais at the front, but currently all the mingling was happening at the back of the room, where connoisseurs, collectors and various hangers-about were milling around, sizing each other up in preparation for the bidding battles ahead.

Arthur, the leading world expert in Things That Go Wrong When Maurice Is Around, had to forcibly restrain the chef from picking up an auction paddle. This was the kind of room in which a badly timed sneeze could easily result in your being the lucky new owner of a thirty-thousand-pound bottle of wine, along with a great deal of sudden debt.

PC Alistair had left them after The Hansdowne Club to go relay the news of Bertie's sudden inheritance to PC Lucy, and to also go check out matinee show times for *The Sound of Music*.

"So tell me, Maurice," said Arthur, "why are we at a wine auction?"

"Aha. In the solving of crime, it is important to know as much about the victim as you know about the murderer."

"Well, that's easy, given we don't yet know the foggiest about the murderer."

Chef Maurice ignored him. "There are many in this room who knew Sir William well. And also a possible suspect." He nodded towards the dais, where Resnick was fussing about with his notes in preparation for his key role.

From over the other side of the room, Mr Mingleberry waved his paddle at Arthur and Chef Maurice and hop-scotched his way through the crowd to meet them.

"Twice in one day, our stars must be aligning!"

"Our pleasure, Monsieur Mingleberry. You come to place a bid?"

"What? Oh no, I just come along to these things for the nibbles and a good old natter. It's a good chance to meet face-to-face with my clients— Ah, speak of the devil, here's one coming by just now." Mr Mingleberry used his cane to hook the elbow of a large rotund gentleman in a pinstriped suit.

"Mr Norton, I didn't know you were in town! Come, let me introduce you to Mr Wordington-Smythe and Mr Manchot. Arthur, Maurice, this is Mr Frank Norton, owner of the Terra Brava Vineyards in Oakville, Napa Valley."

They shook hands.

"We happened to meet one of your fellow countrymen and winery owners the other day," said Arthur. "I suppose you're well acquainted with Chuck Paloni, given that you're both out in Napa?"

Mr Norton's pug-like features descended into a scowl. "Can't say I like his type much. Bunch of johnny-come-latelies, if you ask me."

"The Norton family have been winemakers in Napa since before the Prohibition," explained Mr Mingleberry. "They have, ahem, views on the latest spate of celebrity-owned wineries."

"We'll run them out of town soon enough," said Mr Norton, with some satisfaction. "Not that we need to, in that Paloni's case. I heard Basking Buffalo's not exactly rolling in funds at the moment. Investor troubles. Typical. Hype dies down and then what've you got left? Some actor playing winemaker, mismanaging the place left, right and centre, and a fancy label. That's all."

With a nod, Mr Norton resumed his travels through the crowd, tipping his hat and exchanging ribald jokes with various acquaintances.

Chef Maurice watched the large American depart. "Why do the winemakers attend the auctions? Surely they have no need for more wine?"

"Actually, you'll find they rather do," said Mr Mingleberry. "You'll be surprised how often wineries, even the well-known ones, have to come to auction to buy back their older vintages, especially from the lesser years. Harder to find, you see? All this collecting business has only been going on for a short while. Back in the day, wineries used to simply sell off all the bottles they could. There was none of this keeping back of stock that happens nowadays."

Mr Mingleberry tipped his hat and hurried off to politely accost another of his long-time customers, leaving Arthur in the grasps of a dowager-duchess-style lady who was, apparently, a great fan of Arthur's restaurant column, and was not going to let him go until she got an invitation to accompany him on a review one day soon.

"I'm, uh, flattered, but I'll have to check dates with my editor," said Arthur, looking around desperately for backup, but Chef Maurice had drifted off in search of the source of the canapés.

Eventually, Arthur located his friend at the back of the room, standing by a set of swinging doors, ready to pounce as the waiters emerged with fully laden trays.

"Come on, old chap. We better get seats if we want a good view."

A good view in this case was near the back of the room, where they would be able to watch the rise and fall of paddles and the fortunes that went with them.

They shuffled down the row until they found two seats next to a well-dressed silver-haired lady, with the kind of sharp angular features that called to mind a broody eagle.

"So what's your poison?" she said, looking pointedly at the brochure in Arthur's lap.

"Oh, we're just here to observe. First time at auction and all that, don't want to get carried away."

She looked him up and down, then nodded. "You'll have to do. Right, this is how it goes. If you see me bidding over fifty for the magnum of '61 Latour, that's Lot 212"—she held open her brochure—"you're to break my arm, understand? Harold will have a complete fit if he finds me spending any more on wine this month."

"Fifty . . . ?"

"Thousand, of course." She peered around Arthur at Chef Maurice, who was working his way through a bulging napkin of smoked trout blinis. "Maybe I should ask your friend here instead. He looks more like the arm-breaking type."

"Madam, I assure you I am more than capable in the destruction-of-limbs department, should the need arise," said Arthur, who felt his manliness was being impugned. "Though, if I might suggest that my first course of action would be to relieve you of your paddle, rather than anything more . . . irreversible?"

"Oh, very well, if you must. And, please, call me Eugenia."

A jigsaw puzzle of memory went *click* in Arthur's mind. This was Lady Eugenia, wife of Lord Harold Mansfield, peer of the realm whose father had made his fortune in the manufacturing of instant stock cubes.

She gazed down at the brochure and ran a bejewelled finger over the glossy page. "Such impeccable provenance. Straight from the Vandergriff collection, who've had it since the '40s. None of this 'source unknown' nonsense. Don't drink anything if you don't know where it's been, that's my motto. In fact, only last month, Lord Holland—a dear fellow, known him for years—served us up this bottle of '59 Palmer he said he bought off a friend of his wife's cousin's father, some fellow with a long German name—fishy story, I said right away to Harold—and what a horror it was, pure *vinegar*, though of course everyone was too polite to say anything to the poor man. Well, I had a look at the bottle afterwards, and what do you know, it was an utter *fake*. They'd even spelt 'Palmer' wrong! That's what comes, I said to Harold, of not buying your wines through the *proper* avenues."

She paused to take a deep breath, while Arthur blinked, head spinning from the verbal onslaught.

"Yes," Lady Eugenia continued, tapping the brochure again, "this will slot very nicely into my collection. For the right price, of course." She tapped Arthur's arm with her paddle. "Nothing over fifty, remember?"

"Madam, you have my word."

"You make a collection of magnums, *madame*?" said Chef Maurice, leaning over Arthur. "We have a friend, the late Sir William, who also made a fine collection."

"Oh, yes, of course I know about William's collection. He outbid me on quite a few occasions, though he was ever so gallant about it. Now there was a man who knew how to raise a most apologetic paddle when he knew I was beaten. And he'd send me flowers to commiserate. God rest his soul. The nerve of some burglars nowadays! That's why I keep my cellar key down at the bank, and I make sure to tell all and sundry. I tell them, even *I* can't get at my wines without giving Mr Barclays a call."

Lady Eugenia sighed. "Such a dashing man. And such a shame he never married." She gave the pair an arch look. "Not that I didn't try to stake my claim, back in the days before I met Harold. But William was simply hung up on Annabel Marchmont back then, and then she went and made a complete hash of the thing. Married the wrong man, everybody always said. It should have been William. But in those days, what could you do? He never got over it, if you ask me."

Chef Maurice looked over at Arthur and mouthed, 'A for Annabel?'

"Was Sir William still in acquaintance with this Madame Marchmont?" asked Chef Maurice.

"Oh, no. She died in a road accident—awfully tragic— why, almost ten years ago. Right, hush now, I think we're starting . . . "

The auction proceeded at a steady rhythm, Resnick leading the room like a seasoned circus ringmaster. International collectors rang in their bids, men in dark suits and darker glasses with wires in their ears raised paddles on behalf of their mystery employers, and new records were set for the prices of certain rare old bottles.

The magnum of '61 Latour went for sixty thousand pounds.

"You tried your best, dear," said Lady Eugenia, patting Arthur on the arm. He was massaging a spot on his temple, where the paddle had hit him repeatedly as he'd tried, in the most gentlemanly of manners, to wrestle it out of Lady Eugenia's iron grip when the bidding hit over fifty-five thousand pounds.

"You have my profuse apologies for not succeeding in my duty," said Arthur.

"Nonsense! Sixty was a bargain for that bottle. Even Harold will see that. Now, I've just seen Lady Harwick, I really must go say hello . . ."

Arthur watched her shuffle away down the aisle, still rubbing his forehead.

"Do not worry, *mon ami*," said Chef Maurice. "We have another auction to attend."

"We do? I thought you were just saying that to annoy Resnick."

"*Non, non*, it is real. But you will not be required to stop any bidding. Because, at this one, I intend to win!"

Patrick sat at the long kitchen bench. He was waiting for a batch of puff pastry to chill, while keeping an eye on the spinach-and-feta quiches in the oven, plus making sure Alf didn't lose a finger while boning out a tray of quails. Given this relative lull in activity, it seemed the perfect time to indulge in a little online shopping, in preparation for what he was dubbing The Lucy Project.

"What do you think about this coat?"

Dorothy, who was ironing a stack of starched napkins, looked over. "Oooo, that's a nice one. Reminds me of the one my granddaddy had. He used to practically live in it. Hid the tea stains like nobody's business, it did, and it took three of us together to get him out of the thing to send it to the cleaners."

"Right." Patrick clicked onwards. "How about this one?"

"Ooo, that's a nice one, too."

"If you're a flasher," said Alf, wandering past.

"You know," said Dorothy, tipping her head to one side, "I think you may be right."

Click.

"Nah, mate, only plonkers wear coats like that. And it's *purple*."

Click.

"Now *that's* a fancy coat, luv. Always thought frills would look good on you."

Patrick turned to face his two co-workers.

"Are you trying to help me or not?" he demanded.

Alf, smirking, returned to his quail station.

"We are trying to help, luv," said Dorothy, smoothing out another napkin. "But do you really think that stalking the poor girl is the right way to go about things?"

"I'm not going to stalk her. I'm just happening to turn up in the same place at the same time. I want to get a good look at this other guy."

He didn't dare mention the other part of his plan. He had a feeling that Dorothy would not approve, and Alf would tell him he was just being a plonker.

It was this part of the plan that necessitated a new wardrobe.

In a way, being a chef was a little like being in the army; you had a strictly dictated uniform, you didn't get much of a social life, and there were always men with dangerously sharp objects in your vicinity. It also meant you didn't develop much in the way of outside-of-work wear, seeing as most of your waking hours were spent in chefs' whites.

Eventually, he selected a grey-brown wool blend coat, classically cut, with a dash of the debonair—or at least that was what he hoped.

It occurred to him he wasn't thinking in an entirely rational manner. But everyone said that love was irrational. Therefore, thinking irrationally meant that this was love.

QED.

Heartened by this thought, he hovered over the 'buy' button.

Click.

"I suppose congratulations are in order," said Arthur, as they joined the crowds spilling out of the Smithfield Annual Turkey and Goose Auction.

Chef Maurice, who was pushing a large styrofoam box on a trolley, beamed. "It is a most handsome goose. The Elmore Society will be honoured to have this goose for their Christmas table."

"You do know you're barely going to break even on that dinner."

"Sometimes, *mon ami*, one must think of more than profit!"

"Wait until Patrick sees this monster."

Patrick had long ago taken over doing the restaurant's accounts, after realising that his boss's approach to finances was exactly the same as his approach to making a perfectly seasoned steak tartare—you kept playing around with the amounts until it all balanced out. Unfortunately, this method did not generally sit well with Her Majesty's Revenue and Customs department.

"Patrick," said Chef Maurice huffily, "is not head chef."

He navigated the trolley over a particularly bumpy patch of cobblestones and turned up St John's Lane, which had been recently colonised by several chic eateries and cafes.

He came to a sudden halt. "Arthur! *Regarde.* It is Monsieur Gilles!" He pointed across the road to a small, nondescript coffee shop. In the window, wearing a black coat and a furtive expression, was Sir William's butler.

"Butlers are allowed days off too, I'm sure," said Arthur. "Can you see who he's with?"

But the bold lettering across the front window obscured the face of the man sitting opposite Gilles. Chef Maurice and Arthur watched as the butler reached into his coat and withdrew a rectangular item wrapped in brown paper, about the size of a photo album. He handed it over the table, where it was received by two gloved hands. The unidentified man then stood up and nodded at Gilles.

Chef Maurice gave a yelp and grabbed hold of Arthur's arm.

"It is him! The man who attacked me at Bourne Hall, the night of Sir William's murder!"

The tall man with the white-blond crew cut was now exiting the cafe, fiddling with the clasp of his briefcase. He then set off down the road at a brisk pace.

"*Allons-y!* We must follow him."

"Well, I don't know about *must*," said Arthur, but Chef Maurice was already hurrying across the road, trolley bouncing along in front of him. A red double-decker bus blared its horn as it narrowly missed flattening the pursuing chef.

Up ahead, the blond man continued on, oblivious.

"What about Gilles?" whispered Arthur, as he struggled to keep up.

Chef Maurice stopped and turned around. The top of Gilles's hat was just disappearing around a corner.

"Bah, we know where to find him. But this other one . . . "

"Fantastic, let's leave the butler and follow the heavily armed mystery man instead," muttered Arthur as they hurried on.

Indeed, this would, later on, turn out to have been their first mistake.

Their target had now reached the main road and joined the queue to board a waiting bus. Thankfully, he climbed the stairs to the upper deck, while Arthur and Chef

Maurice manoeuvred the goose trolley into the open bay next to the winding stairwell.

"Excuse me!" said a voice behind them, in tones that suggested imminent warfare rather than apology.

They turned to find a well-dressed grandmother, silk scarf knotted around her neck, with a pushchair full of two-year-old toddler.

"This space is for wheelchairs and buggies!" she said, moving forward an inch to suggest that the battle charge was about to commence.

Chef Maurice looked at her, looked at the little boy, then back up at her. "But this too"—he patted the styrofoam box—"is a buggy."

"No, it isn't," snapped the grandmother, while her grandson gazed up at the big white box.

"Can I havva ride?"

"*Certainement!*"

Before anyone could object, Chef Maurice had scooped up the little boy and placed him atop the trolley's little basket. The toddler looked around the bus, eyes wide at this chance to see the world from up above.

The grandmother opened her mouth, but Chef Maurice nodded at her and said, "See, *madame*, there is now space for you to fold the buggy."

The nearby commuters were silent behind their newspapers, but Arthur could feel the tension of a dozen strangers waiting on tenterhooks for the grandmother to make her next move.

"*Oooopla!*" said Chef Maurice, grabbing the little boy as the bus came to a sudden stop. Passengers shuffled down the stairs and towards the exit, including the blond man, who stared out of the bus window impatiently.

"Sorry, *mon petit*, we must now go." He dumped the boy back into his grandmother's arms and hurried for the door.

It took the combined efforts of Arthur and Chef Maurice to lift the trolley to the ground, and by the time they were back on the pavement their target was a good distance ahead.

Chefs are used to making split-second decisions. After all, it only takes a second for a hollandaise to curdle, a duck breast to go from pinkly juicy to overcooked. In addition, head chefs, especially those in the mould of Chef Maurice, are used to having their words obeyed without question.

The two facts combined possibly explain Chef Maurice's next move, which, incidentally, would turn out to be the second mistake of the day.

He cupped his hands around his mouth. "Stop right where you are!"

The man turned, gave them one look, and took off down a side street.

Chef Maurice swore, fixed his grip on the trolley's handle, and accelerated forwards along the pavement.

As has been noted previously, chefs are not generally built for long-distance running, and their quarry had a good thirty-metre head start.

Arthur would later point out that their progress also hadn't been helped by bringing along several kilos of frozen goose.

Eventually they came to a stop down a blind alleyway, panting and wheezing.

"He has disappeared!" said Chef Maurice indignantly.

"Maybe he . . . went over . . . the wall," breathed Arthur, though he cast a doubtful look at the barbed wire over the brickwork. "Are you . . . sure . . . he came down here?"

"I am most certain."

"Well, then maybe . . . " Arthur's gaze settled on the back door of the red-brick building to their right. It sat just half an inch open, the latch not having caught fully. Beside the door, a keypad gave a little beep of distress.

"But probably best not to—" he began, but Chef Maurice was already barrelling through the door, goose first.

A few moments later, alarms blaring and red lights flashing, they were surrounded by serious-looking men in dark uniforms.

They later agreed that entering the building might have been a bit of a mistake.

If so, that would have made it the third one of the day.

PC Lucy sat down at the end of the train carriage, with Hamilton in his hamper on the seat beside her, and tried not to make eye contact with the other passengers. Apparently her police uniform made her the general face of Authority in these parts, and so far she'd been subjected to twelve complaints about the rising rail fares, nine gripes about delays and cancellations, two requests that she arrest the Minister of Transport and make him ride 'his own effing trains', and one plea to locate a child's toy bunny that had been left on the 10.46 to Brighton last year and had never been returned, despite several strongly worded letters.

Then she'd tried to give up her seat to the wizened old lady who'd got on at Reading, bent double by the weight of half a dozen shopping bags. The woman had looked mortally offended, and now stood swaying in the aisle, throwing PC Lucy the occasional dirty look.

Somewhat surprisingly, Hamilton's presence on the train had caused no more than the occasional surreptitious glance from behind the rows of newspapers. Commuters were clearly a hardened bunch, for whom it would take a lot more than a snuffling pink snout to cause comment.

Her phone buzzed, and several commuters narrowed their eyes at her as she dared to pick it up.

"Hello?" she whispered. "PC Gavistone here. I'm on a train."

She listened for a while to the gabbled voice at the other end of the line.

"Sorry, Arthur, I didn't quite catch that, you broke in where?"

More gabbling.

"Why on earth would you break into the Metropolitan Police Art Fraud departme— Ah. Well, that explains . . .

well, not very much. No! Don't pass me over. I don't want to speak to him."

She wondered briefly if there was a way to arrest Chef Maurice for being a Bloody Public Nuisance.

"Okay, fine, I'll speak to the Superintendent."

A short conversation with the Superintendent of the Art Fraud Unit ensued, in which she confirmed that she did indeed know of a certain Mr Manchot and Mr Wordington-Smythe and, no, they were not known to be art criminals of any description. She considered asking the Superintendent to keep them there overnight as punishment, but decided against it, if only for Patrick's and Alf's sakes. December was a busy enough period for the restaurant, without their head chef being temporarily behind bars.

She hung up and let out a big sigh. Today had not been the most fruitful of days. Paloni had been closeted away somewhere by his PR team, doing interviews for his new film, while Resnick's secretary had refused point blank to give out any information, only stating that his boss was out of the office 'on business'. She'd had PC Sara look into Resnick's financials for any motives hidden there, but the wine critic had come out clean as a whistle. Auction records indicated he'd been earning a hefty sum each year through the commission on Sir William's various purchases, a trend that had showed no signs of abating. If anything, the man would have had a strong motive for keeping Sir William alive and wine collecting for as many years as possible.

As for the Lafoutes, the news of Bertie's inheritance certainly threw a new light onto the case, but it was going to take more than one dusty handkerchief to convince her that wobbly-chinned Bertie Lafoute was capable of cold-blooded murder. Now his wife, on the other hand . . .

Her phone buzzed again, and she groaned when she recognised the number.

"Hi, how's it going? . . . Yes, of course we're still on for Sunday. Did Fred confirm he can make it too? . . . Okay, great— No, don't come round, I'm absolutely knackered, I've been up in London all day . . . Yes. Okay, see you then. Love you too."

She shut her phone and closed her eyes.

"Why does life have to be so complicated?" she asked the world in general.

Hamilton, tearing himself away from a staring match with the five-year-old girl in the seat opposite, gave her a look that said she'd brought this all upon herself, didn't she know that?

I know, she thought. But not for much longer. She'd sort out everything on Sunday; then there'd be no more lies. All she had to do was avoid Patrick until their date next Tuesday. With the hours he worked, and the Sir William case keeping her busy, how hard could that possibly be?

CHAPTER 13

The next morning was not a morning for good news.

Patrick, having been apprised of Chef Maurice's recent poultry expenditure, disappeared into the restaurant's little back office and came out half an hour later with dark pronouncements about cash flow tightening, reduced profitability, and, putting this all into terms that his boss might understand, the potential slashing of January's cheese budget.

This was followed by a call put through to Bourne Hall, which revealed an even more alarming discovery. Gilles had vanished, along with several extremely valuable bottles from Sir William's cellar.

"Well, I guess that's it, then," said Dorothy, who was at the kitchen table polishing the cutlery. "It was the butler who done it. Funny job, when you think about it, being cooped up in that big house all year, 'xcept when Sir William took off to France for his holidays."

"A paid-for annual holiday to France sounds all right to me," said Patrick.

"But it does not make sense!" said Chef Maurice, who was occupying the other end of the table, taste-testing three venison dishes that Patrick was trying to get onto the menu. "If Monsieur Gilles was the one to attack Sir William, why does he choose a night when there are many guests who might witness the crime?"

"He might have been trying to spread the suspicion around," suggested Patrick.

"And also, it is *impossible*! Monsieur Gilles was all the time with me and Arthur."

"But he had an accomplice, right?" said Alf, who was flipping through his new wine book. "The American hitman who was here, the one you chased through London yesterday?"

"But that man, he did not come to Bourne Hall until *after* the crime," said Chef Maurice, stabbing another slice of venison with his fork. "So he also cannot be the murderer."

"Then why was he there?" said Patrick.

"Perhaps to meet Monsieur Gilles? It is clear they are in a co-operation of some type."

"Did Mrs Bates say which wines he stole?" asked Alf, ready to put his newly acquired wine knowledge into action.

Chef Maurice shook his head. "She says they cannot know. He stole the cellar book also."

"Shameful," said Dorothy, shaking her head at the butler's audacity.

"Tell me, how on earth does a guy like him get a girl like *that*?" said Patrick, leaning over Alf as the commis chef flipped past the entry on Chateau Lafoute. In the bottom corner, there was a photo of Bertie and Ariane holding up wine glasses as they posed in front of a barrel.

"Forget about getting her, luv. Keeping her, now that's the problem. See the way he's looking at her, but she's looking off somewhere else? Roving eye, she has, I'll put a bet on it," said Dorothy, who had a postgraduate in Body Language Studies gleaned from a lifetime of reading the women's weeklies. "That being said, guess he's not going to have a problem keeping her now, not with him inheriting all those millions. Wonder if she knew all along. Wouldn't put it past a savvy-looking girl like that to do her research . . . "

"Chateau Lafoute," read Alf, "founded in 1779, was for a long time considered one of the more minor Bordeaux chateaux, until its rise to prominence in the wake of the Second World War, followed by a later surge of interest in the 1980s when Bob Barker, renowned American wine critic, anointed the 1986 vintage with a perfect 314 out of 314 on his now iconic wine-rating scale. The chateau, which has been in the Lafoute family since the mid-nineteenth century, is currently owned by Madame Thérèse Lafoute, while day-to-day operations are overseen by her granddaughter Ariane Lafoute, who heads the winemaking team. The long-term cellarmaster—"

"Aha!" Chef Maurice banged the table, sending Dorothy's neatly laid-out cutlery dancing. "Dorothy, what did you say?"

The head waitress looked confused. "I didn't say nothing, chef—"

But Chef Maurice was already pulling on his jacket. "Patrick, slice the gravlax for today's lunch menu, and prepare all the breasts of duck for dinner. The fridge is much too full now that we have Gérard—"

"Oh great, now we've *named* that goose—"

"—and Alf, assemble two game terrines, wrapped with the dry cure bacon. We will press them overnight."

He paused at the back door. "Does no one ask me where I go?" he said, in a rather hurt voice.

His three members of staff looked up from their duties.

"Where are you off to, chef?" asked Patrick, always one to oblige.

"I go," said Chef Maurice, "to discover the murderer of Sir William!" He paused. "I will return in time for staff dinner."

The door banged shut.

"Well, I think it's sweet," said Dorothy, gathering up the cutlery in her apron.

"What is?" said Patrick.

"Him having a hobby and all."

"Solving murders is now chef's hobby?" said Alf.

"Well, as long as he doesn't start causing any, that's fine by me," said Patrick. "I just hope he knows what he's getting himself into . . . "

* * *

173

Lady Margaret lived a twenty-minute drive north of Bourne Hall in an eighteenth-century manor house known as Cleethorpe Park.

"I think I'm starting to suffer from the status anxiety of living in a cottage," said Arthur, as they stood on the front doorstep, admiring the stone carvings. "All these Halls and Parks and Manors. Meryl will soon start insisting we upsize to a castle."

"Is there not a Wordington-Smythe Manor in your family?" asked Chef Maurice.

"Well, there was something of the sort, a few generations back. But my great-uncle had to sell it off to pay some racing debts."

"Ah, the horses. It is sad, *n'est-ce pas?*"

"Horse racing would have been fine. It was the giraffe racing out in South Africa that got Great-Uncle Harry into a pickle. The upkeep of a racing herd can be ruinous, plus they're a devil to steer, always running off the course and getting injured."

The door was answered by a sour-faced housekeeper, who grudgingly let them inside. Cleethorpe Park bore a passing resemblance to Bourne Hall, but was smaller and in far worse repair. The air smelt stale and undisturbed, though Lady Margaret would no doubt have described it as 'antique'.

They found the lady of the house sat in a high-backed armchair by the fire, if such a name could be given to the dull embers in the grate, which looked as if a sudden sneeze might be the death of it all.

"Mr Wordington-Smythe, Mr Manchot, so good of you to come visit. It's criminal these days, how the younger generations neglect their social duties to their elders."

"It is our pleasure, *madame*. It must be hard, *non*, for a lady to live alone like this?" said Chef Maurice, laying on the Gallic charm in thick spreads.

"It certainly is," said Lady Margaret appreciatively. "And getting help these days is quite a nightmare. Everything has become so *dear*. Now Mrs Pollock, she's been with me for over thirty years now, and still, every year like clockwork, bowing and scraping for a wage increase. I said to her, all this inflation is very well and good but I'm not having any in my house, understand?"

"You have a most acute financial mind, *madame*." Chef Maurice coughed. "I wonder if you have had news of the inheritance of Sir William's estate?"

Two red circles blossomed on Lady Margaret's cheeks. "Indeed I have! I've been ringing up that lawyer for days on end. He kept telling me these matters take time to settle, poppycock I told him, and then finally he comes out and tells me it's all gone to Lady Annabel's boy, Bertie!"

Arthur and Chef Maurice managed to feign gasps of indignation. "You were not included in the will?" said Chef Maurice.

"A collection of silver tea trays, Mr Cranshaw told me. And nothing for my boy Timothy, not a single penny! Not a blood relation, he tried telling me. Well, of course I know that, Timothy was from my first husband, rest his soul, but

I made sure he took the Burton-Trent name, and Henry treated him like his own son. And at the end of the day, a nephew is a nephew, I say!"

"It must have come as quite a shock," said Arthur.

"A complete scandal, if there wasn't scandal enough! I was laid up in bed all day, Mrs Pollock will tell you that"—she gestured at her housekeeper, who had stomped in that moment with a tray of tea and biscuits—"I could hardly eat a thing, just cold tea and plain toast was all I could manage. I mean, that little French minx had been hinting at it, but of course I thought she was lying. She looked just the type."

Chef Maurice coughed again politely. "You speak, perhaps, of Madame Lafoute?"

"Of course I am! You know, now I think about it, she must have known all along. I was admiring the Turner that William has hanging in one of the corridors, saying how Timothy has always had a passion for art, and how he'd make sure these masterpieces were displayed in the *proper* manner, not tucked down some dark hallway like William does with them. And that little madam, she looks at me and gives me this smile, like butter wouldn't melt in her mouth, saying I shouldn't necessarily count on everything one day going to Timothy."

Arthur and Chef Maurice shared a look. "So you think it likely that Madame Ariane knew in advance about the will?"

"Knew about it?" said Lady Margaret. "She had a hand in it, mark my words! Coercing a poor old man like William into leaving everything to that lily-livered excuse

176

for a husband of hers. Her and that butler fellow, wouldn't be surprised if he was all mixed up in it somehow. You've heard he's gone into hiding?"

They nodded.

"Never trust a man who walks too quietly, I always told William. And now there he's gone, pilfering who knows what from the cellar—William's pride and joy!—and running off, probably out of the country already, I'm sure. Disgraceful, the way the police are dealing with the whole thing."

Apparently having exhausted this particular vein of ire, Lady Margaret picked up a teacup and stirred in a lump of sugar with studied fury.

"Madame is an excellent judge of character," said Chef Maurice, in such solicitous tones that Arthur looked up in surprise. "Tell me, what are your impressions of the other guests that evening?"

Lady Margaret shuffled herself up straighter in her chair, clearly flattered. "Well, let's see. Charles Resnick, he's a little too fond of his wine and big words, I'd say, but there's no harm in him as long as you keep your cheque-book close. I do remember some years back, there was some funny business in the papers, someone accusing him of selling some wine he didn't actually own—though how you can do that, I have no idea—but nothing much came of it. A case of sour grapes, no doubt."

She allowed herself a little chuckle at her own cleverness.

"Though, him and all those fancy bottles, I dare say he egged William on a fair bit. But at the end of the day, you can't make a man spend money on something he doesn't want to spend it on."

"Quite," said Arthur, with visions of his new four-wheel drive.

"And Monsieur Paloni?"

Lady Margaret leaned forward. "Distinctly *not* a gentleman. I told William as much, the minute I laid eyes on that man."

"You had made his acquaintance before?"

"Oh no, if I'd known I would be dining in company like *that*, I might not have even attended. These movie people, they're not really *our sort*, I told William. It was obvious the man was simply out to get William's money, getting him to invest in some vineyard out in America. I said to Timothy—he lives out in San Francisco, you know—how do you know the land even *exists*? Napa Valley, sounds like a made-up place, don't you think?

"And *clearly* a ladies' man. You just had to look at him, probably goes for all those hair implants and injecting poison into his face and whatnot. The type to wear red silk underwear, and dark glasses in the middle of winter, I'm sure. I told William I was frankly *shocked* that he should have a man like that staying under his own roof."

"This conversation, this took place in the study of Sir William? Monsieur Gilles made mention that you had wished to discuss something with Sir William that day, something most important?"

Lady Margaret gave him a cold look. "I don't quite see, Mr Manchot, why my private conversations should be any business of yours. And I certainly don't approve of William's butler going around reporting who spoke to whom and all that."

"My apologies, *madame*," said Chef Maurice quickly. "I thought perhaps you had chosen to speak to Sir William on a, how shall we say, delicate topic. I had heard rumours, only rumours, you understand, that Sir William had become involved with a lady of an age much younger than him—"

Lady Margaret started spluttering into her tea. It took a moment for Arthur to realise she was laughing. *"William? At his age? Positively not! Everyone knows he never got over Annabel."*

"Yes, we had heard it mentioned," said Arthur. There was a thought niggling him . . .

"*Un moment, madame.* You said that Monsieur Bertie was the son of a Lady Annabel. This is the same Annabel?"

"Certainly. His mother was Annabel Marchmont, quite the society beauty of her time, as they like to say. A silly girl, though, married the wrong fellow and never did a thing about it. And her boy is no better, going and marrying that French fancy of his. She might act like she has all the airs and graces in the world, but winemaking? It's just a fancy name for grape farmers, if you ask me."

"Very good, *madame*." Chef Maurice paused. "I wondered also if we should be able to visit the gallery here at

Cleethorpe Park? Sir William spoke most highly of the family portraits that his brother had collected together. It would be a pleasure to view such distinguished history."

"Of course," said Lady Margaret, with a benevolent smile. "I'll have Mrs Pollock show you up there. I'm afraid the gallery is rather drafty, and my doctor has strictly forbidden me from such exertions."

A few minutes later, having been deposited there by the surly Mrs Pollock, Arthur and Chef Maurice found themselves tracking dusty footprints along the floor of Cleethorpe Park's Long Gallery. Various stately portraits of past Burton-Trents stared down from the walls above them.

"So what exactly are we doing up here?" said Arthur, stopping in front of a portrait of a moustached gentleman in full army regalia.

"Aha. *Regarde, mon ami*, and tell me what you see."

Arthur looked around at the staring faces of Sir William's ancestors. Many were wearing military uniform, and occasionally perched atop a horse—which was a feat in itself, as Arthur had never seen a horse voluntarily stand still long enough for a decent portrait session.

"Let's see . . . Well, Sir William's forbearers certainly fought valiantly for home and country. And sideburns were eminently more in fashion back in those days."

"Pah, you do not use your eyes. *Regarde*, the *ears*."

Arthur swept his gaze from painting to painting. Now that his friend mentioned it, there was a certain sticking-out-ness common in that particular feature of many of the male Burton-Trents.

"And now, see this." Chef Maurice pulled out the copy of *The World's Hundred Greatest Wines* that Alf and Patrick had been looking at earlier.

The resemblance, now pointed out in all its glory, was impossible to miss. If you ignored the weak chin and floppy fair hair, all the other signs were there. The dark eyes, the set of the nose, and of course, those jutting-out ears.

Arthur looked down at the book again. "The ears have it," he breathed.

There could be no doubt.

Bertie Lafoute was Sir William's son.

"Well, that explains a lot," said Arthur, a while later after they'd returned downstairs and managed to disentangle themselves from Lady Margaret's wide-ranging and voluble complaints about her neighbours, her housekeeper, and all of modern society in general. "Makes sense now, Sir William being so attached to young Bertie, the inheritance, and all that. Do you think he knew? Bertie, I mean?"

Chef Maurice shook his head. "I do not think so. Sir William was an uncle figure to him, no more. There was no conflict in his manner with him, as one would expect if he had known the truth of, how do you say, his birth *illégitime*.

"*Non*, the more important question is, which of the *other* guests had this knowledge? See, *mon ami*, as Sir

181

William's son *naturel* and so the most likely inheritor to his fortune, Monsieur Bertie presents a perfect space-goat."

"Scapegoat, I think you'll find."

"*Exactement!* The murderer, knowing of this, seeks to throw us off the scent once more. In the case that the story of the broken window is not believed, they pick one of the many handkerchiefs lost by Monsieur Bertie, and leave it in the hidden stairs where it will be found."

"Or maybe, just maybe, we're missing the obvious answer here. That Bertie Lafoute is our murderer."

"Bah! This, I cannot believe. Unless Monsieur Bertie is much a better actor than we can expect. You saw how the night of the murder overturned him completely."

"Mmm, yes, rather hard to imagine Bertie up on the stage," said Arthur. "But what I don't understand is, if Lady Margaret is right and Ariane knew about the contents of Sir William's will all along, why wouldn't she have told her own husband?"

"*Les femmes*," said Chef Maurice, waving his hands to suggest all enigmas could be easily understood if only one could figure out the inner workings of the female mind.

"And what was that she said about Paloni being after Sir William's money? I mean, if he was looking to raise more funding for his winery, bumping Sir William off was hardly going to help his cause."

"One can never be sure of the artistic type," said Chef Maurice darkly. "He is unstable, capable of anything."

"Says the man who threw a hissy fit the other day because his macarons came out 'too round'," muttered Arthur.

"One does not eat in a place of fine cuisine to have a dessert that appears made by a machine," grumbled Chef Maurice. "But I think we should speak once more with Monsieur Paloni. Lady Margaret gave mention of one thing I found most interesting . . . "

"And how are you planning to swing that one? I don't think one just drops in on Hollywood directors. In fact, they hire hordes of personal assistants just to keep you away from them."

"Ah, but not every person has a famous food critic as his friend," said Chef Maurice, clapping Arthur on the shoulder.

Arthur gave him a dubious look. Like many other chefs, his friend was more than vocal in his opinion that the role of a food critic was to be found several rungs below that of a chocolate teapot tester, in terms of use to society.

So, if Chef Maurice was bringing it up, it could only mean one thing: there was something he wanted, and he needed Arthur to get it.

As Arthur had predicted, Paloni's schedule was packed tighter than a jumbo tin of sardines. But thankfully, when it came to the world of public relations, there were always plentiful strings to be pulled, if you knew how it all worked. The necessary one was identified, and duly tugged upon . . .

It was lunchtime at La Sobriquette, Piccadilly's long-standing dining room of note, and various media types, celebrities and platinum-card-carrying shoppers were tripping through the brass-edged rotating doors, staring with unchecked curiosity at the odd pair currently occupying Table Sixteen, generally agreed upon to be the best table in the house.

Table Sixteen was a circular leather banquet on a raised dais, set just off to the side of the central dining area, affording it a direct view of the entrance (necessary for keeping an eye out for any A-list friends swinging through the doors), along with a sweeping view of the rest of the room (in case you missed a few acquaintances when you were busy admiring your reflection in the polished mirrors around the walls). Lastly, sitting at Table Sixteen granted everyone else in the room the generous opportunity to gaze upon you and your guests in adoration and envy.

The fact that none of today's diners could put a name to the two men up on the dais was currently causing major consternation amongst this veteran crowd of stargazers.

"The tall, thin one," whispered someone at Table Eleven, "I think I've seen him in the papers somewhere. A foreign politician, maybe. Moldova, yes, Moldova, I'm sure of it."

"I don't think tweed and leather elbow patches are quite the look over in Moldova," sniped his dining partner. "Maybe he's one of the minor Royals?" This caused her a worried look, because snubbing a member of royalty, no matter how minor, was just not the done thing. "The big, fat one, though, he's an actor, for sure. Why else would you grow a moustache like that? He must be in the middle of shooting . . . "

Such was the state of affairs when Paloni came strolling through the doors to find Chef Maurice and Arthur sitting at his usual table.

"Quite a coincidence," he drawled, handing his coat to an attentive waiter.

"Not at all," said Arthur, waving Paloni to the seat across from him. "When my editor heard we'd met before, she thought I'd be the best one to meet you for the paper's 'Lunch with . . . ' piece."

In truth, Lisa, Arthur's blond-highlighted, talon-nailed editor at the *England Observer* had been less than thrilled to give up her chance to hobnob with one of Hollywood's major heart-throbs, but Arthur had sweetened the deal by agreeing to take Lisa's parents along on his two-star Michelin review next week—thus freeing her for a date with Liverpool's bad-boy rock star *du jour*.

Plus Meryl had been less than impressed yesterday evening when her husband had returned late from London, not only having missed dinner but making his arrival in the back of a police car. Arthur therefore surmised that a signed photograph from a Hollywood legend would go some way to soothing the current marital friction.

"Maurice, good to see ya again," said Paloni to the chef,

who was deep in a critical analysis of La Sobriquette's à la carte menu.

"Horseradish with the turbot, *non*, that I do not approve of," muttered Chef Maurice.

"So," said Paloni, clasping his tanned hands together as the waitress swanned off with their drink orders, "I guess we better get down to business and talk about *The Dark Aquarium*?"

Arthur and Chef Maurice blinked at him politely.

"That the fish, they bump into the wall a lot?" suggested Chef Maurice.

"Ha ha, that's a good one," said Paloni. "No. So, I like to start with the moment the idea for this film—the *nucleus* of the thought, I like to say—came to me. I was snorkelling down in New Mexico, I have a little place down there, and I saw this amazing angelfish, which turned out, according to my guide, to have the most amazing defensive properties"—he paused to check Arthur was getting this all down—"so, what they do is, if they see a predator coming toward them, they angle their scales in a way that reflects the light around them and makes them completely invisible. Poof! Then I thought, what would happen if a mad scientist crossed this fish with a rogue ultra-elite military unit?"

"A very dangerous plate of fish and chips?" suggested Arthur.

Paloni, clearly unaccustomed to anything but fawning praise, ignored this. "The most lethal soldier ever imagined. One that can disappear with just a moment's thought!"

"Ahh, *magnifique!*" said Chef Maurice, with grand theatrical awe. "To disappear and reappear, just like that!"

"Yeah, you got it!" said Paloni, gratified to finally have an appreciative audience. "And then I thought, what would be the first thing—"

"But there is another way to disappear and reappear," continued Chef Maurice. "You are familiar with the idea of secret passageways?"

Paloni stopped and looked at Chef Maurice with an aggrieved air. "What?"

"You have not yet heard of the secret passageway between the cellar of Sir William and the bookcase outside the guest bedrooms upstairs at Bourne Hall?"

Paloni threw Arthur the now familiar 'what the heck is this chap on about' look, who responded with his usual 'don't ask me, he just followed me here' shrug. Arthur gave Chef Maurice a little kick under the table. He'd have quite liked to get his photo autographed before Chef Maurice started giving the director the third degree.

"I haven't a damn clue about secret passageways. Now, can we get back to my—"

"Then you deny that after you went upstairs after speaking to Sir William, you used this passageway to descend to the cellar to commit murder?"

"What? Of course I didn't!" said Paloni hotly.

"Yet you were most insistent to speak to Sir William when he went downstairs, and you returned in a most angry mood. May I ask what it was you spoke of?"

"It's none of your damn business!"

"Ah, that is a good word, Monsieur Paloni. Because I think it is because of *business* that you wished to speak with Sir William, *n'est-ce pas*? The business of the Basking Buffalo vineyards.

"You told us Sir William was one of your first investors. In fact, he was to give the after-dinner speech at your next meeting of shareholders. But then his attendance was cancelled. Why? Perhaps he did not approve of the recent bad management of the winery and wished to take away his support? It is known that Sir William was most careful with his investments."

"And if he was, what's it to you?" said Paloni, his face now contorted in an effort to appear cool and contemplative in front of the watching crowd below. "Not a reason to murder a man, just because he doesn't like your balance sheet one year."

"It might be," said Chef Maurice. "If the man holds the respect of much of the wine world. There was every chance that such a blow to, how do you say, the confidence of your investors, might be fatal to the vineyard. So perhaps you took steps, to ensure that he would not have the chance to withdraw his funds . . . "

"What a load of—"

"But what if I tell you," said Chef Maurice, leaning forwards, "that I hear it said you were seen coming out from behind the bookcase on the night of the murder. No, I cannot say by who . . . "

Arthur looked at his friend. This, he was sure, was pure fabrication. The question was, to what end?

"Lies! Some crackpot talking garbage to please the press, I see it all the time. And there's nothing they can pin on me, anyway, because if it comes to it, I've got a watertight alibi!"

"*Oui*, you may have, but can you trust Madame Ariane to tell the truth on your behalf?"

There was a moment's shocked silence.

"Wha— How— What did she tell you?" spluttered Paloni, his composure melting away like a summertime snowman.

"It was only a matter of deduction, to know that you and Madame Ariane were involved in *une liaison*, as we say," said Chef Maurice, leaning back comfortably. "You returned from speaking to Sir William in a black mood, and so, of course, she follows her lover upstairs to offer comfort."

"Damn fool of her too. When a man wants to be alone, you should leave him well alone," fumed Paloni.

"But still, you told the police you were in your room by yourself, *n'est-ce pas*? To save the reputation of the lady?"

"Ha! She didn't even give me the chance. Even before the cops turned up, she told me she was going to insist she was with that damp rag of a husband of hers, instead. She'd already made one of those big heartrending confessions to him, promising to go on the straight and narrow—ha, if I had a dollar every time I've heard a gal say that . . .

189

Anyway, she said at the end of the day, it'd be their word against mine. And what's a fella to do then?"

"Hmmm, *très intéressant*," said Chef Maurice, staring up at the gilded ceiling. "But in truth, she was with you all the time? She did not leave the room?"

"Not for a moment," said Paloni. "But, hey, what's this all about? Are the cops trying to put the finger on Ariane? Because if they are, I don't care what she says, I'll make sure they know everything. It's no skin off my nose!"

"*Non, non*, do not exert yourself, *monsieur*, the police are not to be worried about. For now, that is." Chef Maurice grabbed a bread roll, picked up his hat, and stood up. "I thank you for your time, and wish you a success with your film of the dangerous *poisson*."

With that, Chef Maurice left the restaurant, his progress followed by a dozen curious gazes.

Arthur looked over at Paloni, who had the haggard look of a man who'd just run into the Maurice Manchot Questioning Squad. Time to get matters back on track, before Paloni decided to bolt. He pulled a shiny square of paper out of his briefcase.

"I don't suppose I could trouble you for an autograph? My wife, Meryl, she's a huge fan . . . "

Half an hour later, Arthur located Chef Maurice in a little Italian cafe around the corner, polishing off a plate of tiramisu and a double espresso.

"Okay, spill," said Arthur, pulling out the chair opposite.

Chef Maurice lifted up his coffee cup and looked underneath.

"No, I didn't mean— How in the foggiest did you know all that stuff about Paloni?"

"Ah, when one is trained to observe the smallest of details, it becomes the first nature—"

"—second nature, you mean—"

"—to watch and see what one can learn, in the things that people do not say, the things they do not do."

"So, what you're saying is—it was all guesswork?"

Chef Maurice looked affronted. "*Mon cher* Arthur, you have so small a regard for me?"

"How did you know all that stuff about Paloni's business? Don't tell me you're a sudden expert in wine investments."

"*D'accord*, I will admit that *that* part was a task of speculation. But it seemed clear that the only matter of interest to both Sir William and Monsieur Paloni was the question of the investments in his vineyards, which, we learn from Monsieur Norton at the auction, does not go well."

"Okay. And what about him having an affair with Ariane Lafoute? Don't tell me that was all serendipitous guessing too?"

"Ah," said Chef Maurice, looking pleased. "*Non*. Here, we must use the head." He tapped a finger against his own. "We had made the assumption that the note we found in

Sir William's pocket was meant for him and written by Madame Ariane. But what if we were wrong in our first thought? Madame Ariane has already admitted to a private conversation with Sir William in his study, on the history of Chateau Lafoute, she tells us. Why then would she need to leave him a private note? *Non.* The note was written by her, yes, but it was not intended for Sir William.

"Recall the first conversation we had with Monsieur Bertie. He claims to be a bad sleeper, yet he comes to London and he sleeps like *un bébé*? This cannot be! Those who cannot sleep at home, it is not likely that they sleep well in a new bed. And then we have the many sleeping medicines that Madame Ariane carries with her. Monsieur Bertie's deep sleep, and the fact that Monsieur Paloni stays in the same hotel, this cannot be a coincidence."

"So she was drugging her husband so she could sneak off to meet Paloni? Crafty," said Arthur. "So assuming the note we found was meant for him, how on earth did it turn up in Sir William's pocket? We can assume Ariane left it somewhere for Paloni to find, but I really can't see Sir William being the type to go snooping around his guests' bedrooms."

"*Non*, he was not, but his *belle-sœur*, Lady Margaret, she is *exactly* the type to feel that she has the right to look into the rooms of the other guests. Especially the ones she does not like. Remember, she spoke of Monsieur Paloni being a man to wear 'red silk underwear'. She is not the kind of woman to have the imagination for such detail, and yet, she makes such a claim. How? We know already from looking in his luggage that this is what he wears. So it was Lady Margaret, not Sir William, who looked around Monsieur Paloni's room and found the note. She then insisted to speak with Sir William, most likely to show him the note and complain of the type of guests he invites into his house."

Arthur leaned back in his chair, whistling. "Not bad, not bad at all. But where does this leave us with the identity of the murderer? If we believe Paloni, then it can't have been him. He wouldn't have had time before Ariane went up to see him to sneak down to the cellar. And according to him, it can't be her either. Unless they were in it together . . ."

"A possibility, *oui*."

"They could have arranged the whole thing. The argument, the stomping upstairs. And then, icing on the cake, poor old Bertie is wheeled in to provide a suitable alibi to protect his now-penitent wife, not realising that there's a chance she's been up to something much more sinister . . ."

"Very good, *mon ami*. But what if Monsieur Paloni, he tells us the truth? That he and Madame Ariane were in his room all the time?"

Arthur considered this. It seemed a much less dramatic option. Unless . . .

"What if Bertie's not the wet dishcloth everyone thinks he is? He goes upstairs, finds Ariane gone, and decides to seize the opportunity. There's every chance he was lying about having conveniently 'forgotten' about the secret passageway."

"*Oui*, if it is Monsieur Paloni who speaks the truth, then things do not look very good for Monsieur Bertie," said Chef Maurice gravely. "But *non*, it cannot be . . . "

"You still think he's innocent? Because it's all piling up, motive, opportunity . . . Lucy's going to have him down in the cells pretty soon when she hears about all this."

"Then, we must think faster. There is much still about this case that disturbs me. And also, I have a feeling . . . a feeling that we run out of time . . . "

CHAPTER 14

The next few days in Beakley proceeded at their usual leisurely pace.

General consensus amongst the villagers, as reported by Dorothy, was that Gilles the butler was undoubtedly the culprit, probably a covert recruit from an international ring of wine thieves, and had now gone into hiding across the Mexico border.

Patrick pointed out that the Mexico border would take a rather long time to reach from the Cotswolds, and Gilles would have been better off nipping onto a ferry across to France, but his views were pooh-poohed in favour of a more cinematic outcome.

Old Mrs Eldridge, just returned from a seaside stay in Brighton, claimed to have spotted the fugitive butler working incognito as a waiter in the bed and breakfast she was staying at, but given that last month she had telephoned the police at the sighting of a UFO hanging over the village green—which had turned out to be a particularly oddly shaped gibbous moon, half-hidden behind the clouds—this theory was not given much weight.

PC Lucy had made a show of taking down Chef Maurice and Arthur's latest discoveries, with a promise to 'look into matters in due course', but no further developments seemed forthcoming from the Cowton and Beakley Constabulary.

Come Friday, though, the village was shaken out of its beds by the news that the young Lafoutes had temporarily moved themselves into Bourne Hall, supposedly to sort out the estate's legal affairs before returning to Bordeaux.

"Despicable!" was Dorothy's pronouncement on the situation. "Sir William's hardly cold in his grave and they're probably selling off the furniture and putting in a swimming pool."

Chef Maurice glanced out of the window. The trees were bare and there was a light coating of frost on the hedgerows. Swimming pools, he was sure, could not possibly be on anyone's mind in the current climate.

Still, the return of the Lafoutes now gave him a reason to go back up to Bourne Hall for another look around, especially in the wake of Gilles's disappearance.

It was clear that there were still many missing pieces in this puzzle, and it was high time to start searching under the metaphorical sofa.

Or something like that, anyway.

* * *

"Still refusing to believe good old Bertie is involved in all this?" said Arthur, as they pulled up the long driveway. The snow had melted down to a thin mottled blanket, and tufts of green were poking out here and there in the weak winter sunlight.

"There is no guilt without proof," replied Chef Maurice, staring out over the empty lawn.

"And what about Gilles? No cunning explanation about his disappearance yet?"

"*Non*, but it is possible that he too has become a victim of the murderer."

Arthur rolled his eyes. "So, I take it you'll just be spouting more ominous nonsense in the meantime, until you figure it all out?"

Chef Maurice patted his friend's arm. "It warms me, *mon ami*, that you too are confident that I will, as you say, figure this out."

Arthur sighed, and wondered what life would feel like with an ego as large and impervious as the one owned by Chef Maurice.

There was a shiny Mercedes parked beside the front door, presumably hired by the newly minted Lafoutes.

The bell was eventually answered by a highly flustered Mrs Bates, her hair flying out of its bun and a notepad in one hand.

"Mister Maurice, just who I needed to see! And Mister Arthur too, do come along in." She grabbed them each by an elbow and hurried them down the hallway towards the kitchen. "Dinner for ten, and only a day's notice! Sir William, he always made sure to give me at least five days' warning, four at the very least. It's not like I can conjure up a multi-course dinner out of an empty larder, what with no one having been here the last week, and not knowing what would happen to this place. I wasn't going to go wasting money filling the pantry for no one to eat it up."

"They're having visitors already?" said Arthur.

"Not just visitors. A whole wine-tasting dinner! Inviting up all those fancy critics from London. Such bad taste, like dancing on the poor master's grave, I said. But Mister Bertie was insistent. Though I'd bet he's been put up to it by that French missus of his. She was talking about how it would raise the status of the chateau, having all those la-di-da wine snobs come up here to taste their wines. And so I said, what do you want to serve, and you know what she said? *I* should decide! The master, at least he always had one or two ideas, and of course I knew his tastes like they were my own. But for these two . . . "

The kitchen table was a mess of cookbooks, handwritten recipes, and menu cards from past dinners thrown by Sir William over the years.

"And what with poor Gilles gone and disappeared like that, heaven knows what terrible things have happened to him . . . "

"So you don't share the opinion that Gilles was involved in some way with it all?"

Mrs Bates looked ready to ding Arthur across the head with a copper pan. "How dare you! Gilles has been nothing but devoted to Sir William, from the moment he set foot in the Hall. Always keeping an eye out for him. And Sir William, he trusted him more than any other soul in the world."

"My apologies. So was it a shock to you, when you heard Sir William had left everything to young Bertie?" asked Arthur, keen to steer the conversation away from the contentious butler issue.

"Could have knocked me down with a goose feather, you could've!"

"Ah, so it was expected that Sir William would leave everything to Lady Margaret, or perhaps her son?" asked Chef Maurice.

Mrs Bates cocked her head. "That boy of hers, Timothy? Well, he isn't a *real* Burton-Trent, I expect you know that, and in my opinion, Sir William didn't think much of him and the crowd he ran with. Was quite pleased when he went off to America, I think. Not a *gentleman*, in my mind.

"No, we always thought, Gilles and I, that it'd all go to the charities. The master was always giving donations to this one and that. Of course, there's annuities for me and Gilles, that was only right. In fact, Mrs Lafoute, shows she's not all that bad"—she frowned, as if at pains to admit this fact—"wanted to increase my pension, and get me to stay on here a few more years. But what would I do, just me in a big house like this? It's not like they'll be here much, what with their fancy French chateau and all."

Chef Maurice nodded while he leafed through the various menus strewn across the table. "Did Monsieur Bertie say which wines he wished to serve?"

"Mrs Lafoute, more like it," said Mrs Bates, pulling a sheet out of the pile. "They're starting with two whites, then it's all the way up through the reds. And all Chateau Lafoute, of course."

She handed Chef Maurice the piece of paper, which bore the now familiar curly hand of Ariane.

1848 ("*Mon dieu!*" exclaimed Chef Maurice.)

1901

1913

1928, in magnum

1945

1961, in magnum ("*Oui*, a very good year.")

1966, in magnum

1985

. . . and so on, fifteen wines in all.

"Like drinking a piece of history," said Arthur, with a certain amount of envy.

Chef Maurice stared at the list with an intense look of concentration, his lips moving. After a while, his hand shot out.

"Pen!"

He spent a while scribbling on the back of a menu, with the occasional emphatic crossing out, and mutterings on the line of "*non*, too much lamb, perhaps a fish with the strong flesh, *oui*, that will go." Eventually, he handed the finished product over for Mrs Bates' inspection.

She ran an appraising eye down the list. "Very nice," she said, nodding. "These three dishes, I can pre-prep them, so no problems there, good mix of flavours but nothing too overpowering. The timing's good as well, no fighting for oven space. Still," she added, drawing out the word as she gazed around the kitchen, "it's a mighty big task to get it all done tomorrow by myself, by the time I get the deliveries in and all . . ."

Chef Maurice, always highly attuned to a cook's way of thinking, took the hint. He was faultlessly generous with his time when it came to those in need.

He was, also, faultlessly generous with everyone else's.

"I will send to you my commis chef," he said grandiosely. "*En tout cas*, Le Cochon Rouge is closed tomorrow. My sous-chef has asked for the evening off," he added with a dark look.

"I see you didn't volunteer your own services," said Arthur, as they headed down into the wine cellar in search of the new master of the house.

"I would, *mon ami*, but I expect to be occupied to-morrow evening."

"Really? With what?"

"The dinner, of course. It is most important that I attend. An idea comes to me . . . I think we become nearer to the solving of the crime. But there are things I must make certain first."

"Like whether or not you're invited?"

"*Mon ami*, one does not wait to be invited. I will arrange my own invitation."

"Of course," muttered Arthur. "So you think you're on to something?"

"Ah, perhaps I speak too soon," said Chef Maurice, rubbing his moustache. "But when I have made an arrangement of my ideas, I may require your help."

Arthur groaned. "I had a feeling you might say that." He turned his thoughts to more solvable mysteries. "It's not like Patrick to ask for a day off. I wonder what he's up to tomorrow?"

Patrick sat at the little desk in the cramped office of Le Cochon Rouge, pen and squared paper at the ready.

He'd been back and forth with himself about this part of the plan, but so far a better alternative had yet to present itself.

Still, he was loath to commit pen to paper and part with a recipe he'd been working on for several years. It had won him first place in the Regional Young Chef of the Year when he was first starting out, and he occasionally managed to persuade Chef Maurice to put it onto the specials menu, to unanimous rave reviews from their regular diners.

Many of his fellow chefs had begged for this recipe, made attempts to borrow his technique, or, in one particular case, resorted to a bungled attempt at theft—only to find that Patrick had never written it down—but he'd never had a reason to give in to their pleas.

Until now.

Because if he was going to win over the heart of a particular blonde policewoman, he needed all the help he could get.

With a heartfelt sigh, he picked up the pen.

Some ten minutes later, deed done, he folded the paper and slipped it into an envelope. Then he picked up his phone and typed:

It's all yours. See you tomorrow.

They found Bertie at the back of the wine cellar, with a spiral-bound notebook, a pen and a good quantity of dust in his hair.

"Oh, hallo," he said, scrambling up from his knees. "Good of you to visit, didn't realise news would get round so soon."

Chef Maurice pointed to the notebook. "You make an inventory?"

"Afraid so. They tell me Gilles stole the cellar book too, though I can't fathom why. I can't say it was a thrilling read, but at least it was all in there. Location of each bottle, place it was bought, price paid, all that stuff. It's going to be all guesswork now."

"I'm sure the police are bound to catch him at some point," said Arthur. "Damn hard to disappear in this day and age, what with all this CCTV and border control and whatnot."

"I suppose so," said Bertie, not sounding overly concerned. After all, thought Arthur, what was a few stolen bottles compared to the millions now awaiting the young man?

On an upturned barrel in the corner, various exalted vintages of Chateau Lafoute were standing to attention, ready for their debut at tomorrow's big dinner.

"We took them out first thing when we arrived yesterday," said Bertie, "but Charles says he's not sure the sediment will have time to settle. It really should have been done days ago, but of course this was all rather last minute."

"Charles? Charles Resnick?" said Arthur. Trust that man to waste no time insinuating himself into the company of the new master of Bourne Hall.

"Oh yes, this was all his doing," said Bertie, with cheery enthusiasm. "Well, him and Ariane. There was meant to be a big gala dinner in London tomorrow, hosted by the Wine Bureau of Burgundy. But there was an awful fire at the venue, and they had to postpone to next week. So what with all these big-name wine writers in town, Ariane had the idea—or was it Charles, I don't quite remember—anyway, we thought, why don't we have them all up to the Hall for the biggest ever tasting of Chateau Lafoute?"

"Wine, it is meant to be drunk," said Chef Maurice, nodding.

"Right. That's just what Charles said."

No doubt he would, thought Arthur, if it meant he got to be one of those doing the drinking.

"Ariane's very excited. She says she's never even tasted some of these vintages before."

Arthur glanced towards the magnum collection in the glass display case. There were now several more empty plinths, and on the barrel table, he saw that the '28, '61 and '66 magnums of Chateau Lafoute had joined their smaller brethren in anticipation of tomorrow's unveiling.

Chef Maurice was now pottering around the cellar, looking high and low at the bottles all around him. "The stickers!" he said, waving a hand at the shelves. "The yellow stickers. They are all gone!"

"Stickers?" said Bertie.

"There were many bottles marked with the little yellow stickers," said Chef Maurice, his nose now pressed up against the glass of the magnum collection. "Perhaps one in twenty, or one in ten, even, had the mark. See there"— he pointed to a sticky smudge on the edge of a '29 Cheval Blanc—"you can see it has been removed."

"Maybe Gilles took them off, before he left," suggested Arthur.

"*Oui*, perhaps. But why?"

"Maybe he was marking out the ones worth taking?"

"*Non, non*, the stickers, they were here on the night of Sir William's murder. It is impossible that Sir William would not notice. So they must have been put on the bottles with his consent. Perhaps even put by him. Which— Aha! Yes, this fits very well . . . "

Chef Maurice continued pacing up and down, a glazed look across his face, as if concentrating on some inner vista of thought.

Arthur shrugged, and turned to Bertie. "So, master of Bourne Hall, eh? Must have come as quite a shock. Though, you must have had some inkling . . . ?"

Arthur carefully watched Bertie's face, but the young man showed every sign of flustered embarrassment. "Oh no, I didn't have the slightest idea. I mean, looking back, perhaps I should have—I mean, Uncle William did used to say the odd thing or two, usually after he'd been at the Port, about how I was like the son he'd never had, that kind of thing. But I never thought . . . He was awfully keen on the idea of us young people making our own way in the world, not waiting for handouts and all that. And he had family still, at least, his brother's family . . . "

"Mmm, I imagine Lady Margaret had some words to say on that matter."

"She keeps ringing up. I've had to tell Mrs Bates to tell her we're out," said Bertie, looking scandalised at having descended to such a level of subterfuge.

"And how's Ariane taking it all? I don't suppose she had any idea about Sir William's plans? It's funny how women intuit these things, sometimes . . . "

"Ariane? Oh no, she was as shocked as I was. Though I have to say, she got her head around it a lot quicker than I did. She's already got it all earmarked—we've given the go-ahead on the purchase of the new fermentation tanks, and she's going to speak to the builders about the new visitor centre when we get back."

Bertie gave his head a little shake. He wore the bemused look of a man with a wife on a very serious spending spree.

"Will Madame Lafoute, her *grand-mère*, I mean to say, be in attendance at the dinner?" asked Chef Maurice, halting in his circuit of the room.

"I'm afraid not. She's not so keen on flying nowadays, so we're having a little film made instead, at the chateau itself. Ariane's flown down there this morning with Chuck and his film crew."

"Very obliging of him," said Arthur, without thinking. Too late, he noticed the slight flush in the young man's cheeks.

Dammit. Of course, Bertie already knew about his wife's affair—Paloni had said as much. No doubt she had made various conciliatory gestures and promises in the aftermath—after all, surely not even Bertie would be as spineless as to let his wife go gallivanting off with a man she was *still* having an affair with—but even so, the topic was clearly a sore point. And no wonder.

"He did insist on being able to attend the dinner himself. A return for borrowing his film crew, though he didn't say as much," said Bertie. "A bit odd, I said, having another winery owner here, but Ariane had her heart set on capturing her grandmother on film."

"Ah, *c'est terrible*," said Chef Maurice, tutting. "To make such an imposition on you. These Americans . . . " He laid an arm around Bertie's shoulder. "But now that we speak of the guest list . . . "

* * *

"You really are a shameless hussy," said Arthur, as they climbed back into the car.

"Bah! There is no time for making politeness. There is a crime continuing, and I must be there to stop it."

"Oh, come now, you're not honestly expecting another murder at this dinner, are you? And what are you going to do, tackle the perpetrator with a fish knife?"

"Aha, I did not say the crime I speak of will be murder. There are, we know, many other crimes in this world . . . "

Arthur gave up. Getting information out of Chef Maurice when he was in one of these moods was harder than turning water into wine.

"You could have at least got me an invite, too."

"Ah, do not worry, *mon ami*. You are also in my plan. Do not think you will be left on the outside of the loop."

"Oh, goody. Still, at least you've finally seen sense—a cool customer, our Bertie is. I do have to agree with Mrs Bates. Rather bad taste and all, having this party all so soon."

"*Comment?* Ah, you still hold on to your idea that Monsieur Bertie is our murderer?"

"Is there any other alternative? He's got the motive, he's bound to have known about the passageway, and then there's that handkerchief, to top it all off. He's our man, all right."

"*Non, non*, it cannot be. There are still too many questions. What is the purpose of the yellow stickers? Why

208

does Monsieur Gilles disappear? And why this dinner, why now? When we know the answers to all this, only then, *mon ami*, we will have the answer to the murder of Sir William . . . "

That night, Chef Maurice went to bed, a glass of cognac in his hand, his mind whirring.

It all came down to the money, of course, but that wasn't the important part. It was the wine, he was sure of it. Gilles's disappearance, the missing cellar book, even the fact that Sir William had been murdered in his very own wine cellar. Wine was the key to all this.

He remembered that night at Le Cochon Rouge. Sir William walking away, muttering: "*In vino veritas*. Hah, or so I thought . . . "

Chef Maurice had kept hold of *The World's Hundred Greatest Wines* for a little bedtime reading. As he flipped through the pages, his thoughts turned to the task ahead. He was almost certain he now knew who the murderer was. But almost certain wasn't nearly good enough. And then there was the little matter of proof . . .

He reached over to top up his glass and found his bedside decanter empty. With a sigh, he threw back the warm covers and wriggled his feet into the thick woollen socks Dorothy had knitted for him last Christmas. They were made of thick black wool, with grey toes, just like his usual steel-capped boots—though the effect was rather marred by the fluffy pompoms Dorothy had sewn on around the cuff.

In the kitchens, the smell of gently simmering mulled wine drifted about in the dark. But, to his surprise, the room was not in complete blackness. There was a faint light, spreading out from beneath the cellar door.

Either Patrick, who had seemed oddly distracted of late, had forgotten to turn the lights off, or else . . .

Chef Maurice tiptoed over to the pastry section and felt around for the largest rolling pin. Then, woollen socks muffling his footsteps, he eased open the cellar door and peered inside.

A blond crew-cut head was bent over the wine racks. Not just any wine racks, but the section belonging to the late Sir William.

"Hands up, or I shall call the police! And lock you in this cellar, without any wine glasses," added Chef Maurice, in his most menacing tones.

The man stood up slowly, hands on head. "Now, sir, I can explain," he said, in clipped East Coast tones. "This isn't what it looks like."

Chef Maurice waved the rolling pin. "*Non*, in fact, I am hoping that this is exactly what it looks like. Because if you are who I think you are, *monsieur*, then I require your help in the trapping of a murderer."

"And who do you think I am, sir?"

Chef Maurice told him.

CHAPTER 15

It was the evening of the grand wine tasting. Sunday church bells rang faintly in the distance. At the Bourne Hall front door, the chime of the doorbell was answered by a tall gentleman in a black tailcoat.

"Good evening, madam. Do come inside. May I take your coat?"

Miss Janet Fetters, acclaimed critic for the *International Journal of Wines and Spirits*, peered over her glasses at the butler.

"Arthur, is that you, under that . . . *thing*?" She waved a hand at his face.

The butler grimaced and tugged off the fake moustache.

"You don't think it suits me?"

"It looked like it was savaging you."

"I see. Opinion duly noted."

Arthur stuffed the offending face piece into his pocket and led the new guest through to the main drawing room, where a Champagne-fuelled reception was well underway.

Ariane, resplendent in a glittering black dress that clung to her figure for dear life, was flitting around the small crowd, dispensing kisses and effusive thanks for the guests' having travelled all this distance to be here. Lady Margaret sat on the long sofa, watching disapprovingly as yet another bottle of Champagne was popped—something she no doubt viewed as the flagrant squandering of Timothy's rightful inheritance.

Resnick was standing by the fire in the middle of a coterie of his fellow wine writers, which included the colossal form of Bob Barker, America's foremost wine critic. A perfect score of 314 from him could send a wine rocketing off the shelves all around the globe, and 'Barkering a wine' had become a common catchphrase for setting out to create the light, fresh, high-acidity wines so favoured by Barker himself.

Bertie Lafoute stood off to one side, an untouched glass in his hand, watching the milling guests with an odd, almost calculating stare. It was momentary, though, and his usual expression of bemused good-naturedness returned as he spotted Arthur and hurried over.

"Everything going all right?"

"Very good, sir," replied Arthur, endeavouring to play the part, even if he was *sans* moustache.

"Good, good. Honestly, I can't say how grateful we are for your stepping in like this, makes the whole thing run so much smoother, and Mrs Bates already had so much on her plate." He looked down at his watch. "I think everyone's here now. Maybe you could send in the rest of the canapés, then we'll move through to the dining room after?"

"Certainly, sir," said Arthur, and glided away towards the kitchen.

He found Mrs Bates loading up the final trays with little jewel-like creations—duck pâté with cranberries on slivers of melba toast, delicate goat's-cheese-and-honey crostini, and of course, the little Yorkshire puddings so beloved by Sir William.

The hired waitstaff had failed to materialise, citing bad weather and a faulty minivan, so Alf had been hastily transferred from commis chef duty to front-of-house, courtesy of one of Gilles's old suits. He now hovered nearby, itching at the collar of the ill-fitting white shirt, complete with a slightly lopsided bow tie.

"Off you go now," said Mrs Bates, pushing a finished tray towards him.

"Dorothy makes this look so easy," muttered Alf, his knees buckling as he heaved the tray onto one shoulder and weaved his way out of the kitchen with only minor damage to the doorframe.

Chef Maurice, in a black dinner jacket and burgundy-coloured velvet bow tie, was dozing in the armchair beside the stove.

Arthur prodded him with his foot. "Late night yesterday?"

Chef Maurice opened one eye and looked up at his

friend. "Ah, that is much better. The moustache, it did not become you, *mon ami*. I trust you have not lost it?"

Arthur patted his pocket. It had been Chef Maurice's idea, after listening to Arthur's concerns of being recognised, for his friend to borrow the disguise. Though why a man who already had such a monstrous one of his own should own a fake moustache was beyond Arthur's comprehension.

"Did you know Lady Margaret would be here? I thought she doesn't even like wine—she only ever came to these things to butter Sir William up. And that didn't exactly work out."

"Perhaps she now chooses to make her appeal to Monsieur Bertie himself. He tells me that she, also, had made her own invitation. See, *mon ami*, to do such things is not unusual, even for the English."

Only if they're crotchety old ladies with an eye on a hefty inheritance, thought Arthur. Though the chance of Lady Margaret guilt-tripping Bertie into handing over some of Sir William's fortune was unlikely, what with Ariane's winery-expansion plans.

There was a commotion out in the hallway, then Paloni appeared in black-tie, flanked by a cameraman and soundman.

"Just getting some footage of the preparations," he said, eyeing up the kitchen from between two squared hands. "Now, Arthur, if I could get you to step aside, and Mrs Bates, try to look busy . . . "

"I *am* busy," muttered Mrs Bates through gritted teeth, as she piped cream cheese into the smoked trout parcels.

"Fantastic! Very atmospheric. Come on, boys, let's go get some shots of the big gallery upstairs . . ."

Paloni and his crew trooped off again, leaving the kitchen in relative peace.

"That man should be ashamed of himself," said Mrs Bates, moving on to the next tray. "Do you know what he was up to earlier? He had some actor man all dressed up like Sir William, wandering all about the garden! Said he wanted to capture the history of Bourne Hall. Well, I think it's completely tasteless. Had no thought at all for my feelings. Gave me such a turn, like seeing a ghost, it was. He looked ever so like him, especially when he turned his head just so."

Arthur looked over at Chef Maurice. "I'm surprised you're not out there hobnobbing, old chap. What with all the fizz and canapés floating around."

Chef Maurice reached down wordlessly and hefted up a half-empty Champagne bottle from under his chair.

"And why do you think it's taking me so long to load up all these trays?" complained Mrs Bates. "He keeps snuffling up the canapés when he thinks I'm not looking. And with a five-course dinner to follow as well, I don't know . . ."

There was a little squeak from under Chef Maurice's armchair. Arthur bent down. It was Hamilton, sat in a little basket with a tartan blanket, a silver platter of sow nuts beside him.

"Should he even be in here?"

"I thought *le petit* Hamilton should not miss out on the evening. If things happen as I plan, I assure you they will be most spectacular."

"I do hope you're not planning any fireworks, Mister Maurice," said Mrs Bates distractedly. "Scares me no end, all those big bangs."

"Do not worry, Madame Bates, there will be none of *those* type of fireworks."

Alf staggered back into the kitchen with an empty tray and a harrowed look in his eyes. As Mrs Bates readied another tray for the following salvo, he sidled up to Chef Maurice.

"Delivered your message, chef."

Chef Maurice's eyes sprang open, suddenly alert. "*Oui?*"

"She said to meet up in the Pinky Mauve Room, chef. And you better make it quick."

Chef Maurice stood up and brushed a few crumbs from his lapels.

"Stay here and guard the kitchen," he said, addressing the hidden Hamilton. He nodded at the others. "I will return soon. Tonight, a murderer will be revealed."

Patrick got off the bus in Cowton's town centre, just across the road from Trattoria Bennucci. It was starting to snow again and little flakes were settling on his new hat, which, the shop lady had assured him, gave him the look of a young Gregory Peck. Whoever that was.

His new scarf was tied just so around his neck in a way that *Gentlemen's Weekly* claimed would impress 87.4 per cent of girls he met, and a single purple iris was clenched in one gloved hand as he contemplated his next move.

Either Lucy would look at him in a completely new light after this evening, or it would all go hideously wrong and she'd never speak to him again. But wars were not won, he told himself, by coming second.

Through the big glass frontage, he could catch a glimpse of her, sat at a table in the middle of the room. She was alone, gazing around with a bored expression and perusing the menu in the manner of someone who had made their choice ten minutes ago and now regrets having bothered to turn up on time.

It was now or never.

He crossed the road, took a deep breath, and pushed open the door.

In the Pinky Mauve Room, Ariane was seated at the little vanity table, powdering her nose from a compact. She looked up in the mirror as Chef Maurice entered quietly.

"Thank you for allowing me this meeting, *madame*."

Ariane turned to face him. "Tonight is an important night for Chateau Lafoute. Please make this quick. I must return soon to my guests."

Chef Maurice wandered over to the tall bay windows. It was dark outside now, but moonlight picked out the first shimmer of snow settling in the garden below.

He cleared his throat. "The murder of Sir William has always seemed to me a fantastical one. The method? A secret stairway and a bottle of fine wine. And those held suspect? A group of his most esteemed guests. The discovery of the truth, it has not been simple. And made even less by the many lies told."

Ariane watched him silently from her seat before the mirror.

"You, *madame*, for example, you gave two lies. The first? That you went upstairs on the night of the crime to rest in your own room. But you did not. Instead you went to Monsieur Paloni, who had been in some anger after his conversation with Sir William."

"Where did you hear such a lie? I was with my husband. He will tell you so."

"Come, *madame*, there is no time for this game. The note you left for Monsieur Paloni, it was found by the police. I am certain it can be proved to be your hand-writing, if you so wish."

Ariane gave a shrug of her thin shoulders.

"And then, we come to your second lie. You say to your husband that you are shocked to hear of his inheritance. But this is not true, *n'est-ce pas*? You are an observant woman. You had already made the guess that Sir William was Monsieur Bertie's true father. It could be presumed that Monsieur Bertie would likely come to inherit the estate after Sir William's death. In fact, you could not resist to make such a jibe, as they say, to Lady Margaret."

"I could not be certain about anything. I merely spoke to annoy that horrible old woman."

"Ah. Perhaps you were not certain, but I think that you were sure enough. Enough, perhaps, that it happens like this.

"On the night of the murder, you climb the stairs, saying you retire to your own room. Instead, you go to the bookcase, the secret passageway your husband once talked about in his childhood tales, and you run quickly down the staircase. You carry one of Monsieur Bertie's hand-kerchiefs, so that you may wipe your fingerprints from the bottle after. You stand behind Sir William, and raise your hand. And then . . . "

Chef Maurice brought his own hand down into his other palm in a loud, meaty slap.

"Sir William's death, you were sure, would make your husband a very rich man. And you had many plans for your vineyard. All you needed after was to convince the two gentlemen, Monsieur Paloni and Monsieur Bertie, to both lie for you. Which they do, most admirably. And so you have my tale." He gave a little bow.

"A bizarre story," said Ariane with disdain. "Yes, I asked them to lie for me, I will admit that, but it was only to protect my husband. It was obvious he would face suspicion, if Sir William had left his estate to him as I thought. So I took a precaution. That is all."

Chef Maurice regarded her for a long moment. Then, finally, he nodded.

"And I believe you, *madame.*"

"*Comment?*" Ariane blinked.

"*Oui, ma petite.* I do not believe you would murder Sir William. Not for the money your husband would inherit."

"You can be so sure?" She stuck out her chin, defiant.

"*Oui.* You, *madame*, could have married any of the world's many rich men. Men like Monsieur Paloni, *par exemple*. Yet you make the choice of Monsieur Bertie, a man who had no riches before this week. And why? It is simple. Because you fell in love with him.

"And not just that. You love him still, very much. My friend, Arthur, he is very English. He would not understand. But when you heard of the murder, you sought to protect Monsieur Bertie with an alibi. You did this, not knowing whether he would inherit or not. And not even knowing, *madame, if he was innocent of the crime.*"

Ariane looked at him. "You tell more stories?"

"Ah," said Chef Maurice, shaking his head, "perhaps if there was more time. But there is not. Until the murderer is captured, there are those who still live in danger. I have my ideas, but what I do not have, is the *proof*. And so, *madame*, I ask for your help. If you will give me your permission to, how shall we say, add to the evening's entertainment . . . "

Ariane listened to Chef Maurice's proposal, eyes narrowing as he spoke. Finally, she nodded.

"You have my permission. But this must work. Or you put us all in grave danger!"

220

"It will work. I give you my assurance." Chef Maurice strode towards the door. "I go now to make the final arrangements. Return, *madame*, to the entertaining of your visitors. You may leave the rest to Papa Maurice . . . "

CHAPTER 16

Patrick sauntered past the restaurant reception, keeping his gaze fixed on the back of the room. He was just passing PC Lucy's table when he heard a little gasp and looked down to meet her blue-eyed stare.

"Patrick?" She sounded startled, more confused than guilty, though he saw her gaze flicker towards the front door.

"Oh, hi." He tipped his hat. "Fancy seeing you here. I didn't think this was your kind of place."

"It wasn't my choice," said PC Lucy with a grimace. She appeared to have now recovered from the surprise. "What brings you, er—"

"Just catching up with an old friend," he replied, with painstakingly practised insouciance. "I think I see her over there. I better go sit down. Have a good evening." He tipped his hat again, wondering if two rounds of hat-tipping was a bit overkill, and strolled as slowly as he dared over to the table in the back, which was occupied by a long-legged dark-haired woman wearing a fur-trimmed coat.

"Patrick, *mio caro*, it has been too long," she purred, unfurling herself from her seat to kiss him on both cheeks.

"You too," said Patrick, taking his seat opposite her. He was facing the wall, which was probably a good thing, in that PC Lucy would not be able to see his face. Unfortunately, it wasn't so good for being able to keep an eye on hers.

"Can you see her? What's she doing?" he whispered, leaning over the table.

Isabella glanced up. "She is looking at us. She looks very angry. Do you really think this was a good idea?"

"We're just having dinner. That's allowed, isn't it? Plus, she can't talk. She's definitely meeting some guy here tonight."

Isabella gave a little eye roll. "You men. So territorial. Did you bring the recipe?"

Patrick patted his pocket.

"Perfect. It will go onto my spring menu," she said, with a wicked glint in her eye.

Isabella Raffini was currently making headlines as the youngest ever female head chef to grace the kitchens of a two-star Michelin restaurant, not to mention being by far the most photogenic. The press were swarming all over her, and she had obliged them by posing for one particular photo shoot wearing only a tall white chef's hat and holding a large, but not very large, baking tray. Patrick knew that Alf had a printout pinned up in his room, and would probably keel over with jealousy if he knew Patrick was here with her tonight.

But to Patrick, Isabella had always been just another brother-in-arms, a fellow fighter on the culinary battlefield. They had trained in many of the same kitchens earlier in their respective careers and, in contrast to certain of his colleagues, Patrick had never had any interest in getting any closer. Seeing someone ferociously gut, debone and skewer half a dozen wild ducks in under five minutes on their first day at work could have that effect on a man.

"And you, Patrick, why do you work here in the middle of nowhere? In a village restaurant? You should be in London, it is where things happen. By now, you could have your own restaurant. There are people I could put you in touch with."

"I know. But, well, London always did my head in, and I'm getting to quite like it out here. Honestly. Plus . . . " His thoughts turned to PC Lucy. "Wait, is she still looking?"

Isabella took another glance over his shoulder. "No. But she looks sad."

"Sad?"

He'd expected fury, envy and possibly a well-aimed ballistic truncheon. Sadness hadn't been on the menu.

Isabella held out an imperious hand. "The recipe?"

"Later! We're meant to be pretending to be on a date, remember? Which means *not* looking like a pair of spies swapping state secrets."

"Suit yourself," said Isabella, and converted her gesture into a finger-curl at a nearby waiter, who executed a swift about-turn and zoomed in their direction. She ordered them two glasses of expensive Champagne, which elicited a slight wince from Patrick. Payday wasn't for another two weeks.

"You *did* say this was a date," said Isabella, settling back in her chair. Her eyes lit up as she stared past him. "Ah, now the drama begins."

"Is it him? Is he here?"

Isabella nodded, as she stretched out a hand towards their returning waiter, who placed in it a tall bubbling glass. "He's not much to look at, though," she said, taking a sip. "Thin, not very tall. He seems to be attempting to grow a beard, and failing. Her friend, though, she is pretty—"

She paused. And continued to pause.

"What? What is it?" Patrick fought against every nerve in his body, which desperately wanted to turn around and gawk. "Is he proposing? Tap-dancing? Taking off all his clothes? What?"

Finally, Isabella turned her cool, assessing eyes on him. "Patrick?"

"Yes?"

"I have news for you."

"Yes?"

"You are a giant idiot."

"Yes. But *why*?"

The guests filtered slowly into the Bourne Hall dining room. To Arthur, there was the unsettling feeling of continuation on from the last fated evening when he was in this room, except that tonight he was playing the part of Gilles.

The table was laden with wine glasses—Arthur having laid them out earlier with the help of a metre rule and set square—crystal jugs of water, small plates of plain crackers, and spittoons. The latter were mostly for the show of things; no one had come tonight expecting to do anything but swallow.

The Lafoutes had invited eight guests in total. In addition to Lady Margaret, Paloni, Resnick, and Chef Maurice, the roster included the four most influential wine voices of the decade: Miss Janet Fetters, she of the cat-eye glasses and rapier pen; Mr Bob Barker, jovial and loud, with the physique of a punching bag; Mademoiselle Céleste Dauphine, a young French critic, scion of a notable French wine family; and finally Herr Hunfrid Herrmann, publisher of the celebrated German wine magazine *Wein*.

They took their seats. Paloni wasted no time in unleashing his charms on the unsuspecting Céleste, while Bob Barker and Hunfrid Herrmann exchanged shouted opinions across the table about the latest release of Rheingau Rieslings. Lady Margaret occupied the far end of the table, staring around at her fellow guests with a lemon-sucking expression.

"Quite a journey through the decades," said Miss Janet Fetters, running an eye down the lavishly calligraphed list of vintages.

Chef Maurice, sat to her left, nodded. "They have all come from the cellars of Bourne Hall, I am told," he said, with a glance at Ariane, who was seated at the head of the table.

Their hostess nodded. "Sir William was a long-time admirer of my family's chateau. There were in fact many more vintages downstairs, but Charles and I"—she shot Resnick a brief smile—"thought this list would represent the peak expression of Lafoute across the years."

There was the gentle tap of fork against glass, and the guests quietened down to a murmur.

Arthur took up a suitably butler-ish position by the door. To his surprise, it was not Ariane but Bertie who stood. Perhaps as the new master of Bourne Hall, the young man felt it was his duty to lead the night's proceedings.

"Good evening, ladies and gentlemen, and thank you for being here with us tonight, especially given the short notice. As much as I regretted to hear of the postponement of your undoubtedly stellar Burgundian dinner, I'm afraid I can't be too sad, as it offers us the unparalleled chance to gather here tonight the most distinguished palates of today's wine community, for what is certain to be the most extensive tasting of Chateau Lafoute ever to be held."

Bertie surveyed the table with a level gaze, only the slight bob of his Adam's apple giving away any hint of nervousness.

"I am sure Chateau Lafoute needs no introduction to those present, but as we are unable to be in the vineyards tonight"—a brief smile—"we took the liberty of shooting a short film at the property yesterday, with the help of a friend of the family. A certain filmmaker of note."

He nodded at Paloni, who flashed his megawatt smile around the table.

Bertie pressed a button on a handheld remote and a white screen began to unfurl from high on the ceiling, where it had been neatly concealed by the plasterwork. Arthur stood watching its stately descent—he remembered Sir William boasting about having the screen installed a few years back, along with the purchase of a couple of comfy velvet chairs and a popcorn maker—then noticed Ariane staring at him pointedly, and hurriedly dimmed the lights.

The presentation began with snatches of grainy black-and-white film; a montage showing the chateau and its surrounding vineyards over the years, merging then into a monochrome portrait shot of Madame Thérèse Lafoute, staring out over her domain from one of the chateau's many balconies. Her white hair fanned out in the breeze, and it was clear from whom Ariane had inherited her impressive cheekbone structure.

"History . . . " boomed a deep voiceover, which sounded suspiciously like Paloni speaking down a didgeridoo. "Culture . . . longevity . . . integrity . . . "

The list of dignified nouns rolled on, accompanied by close-up footage of Ariane wandering through the winter vines in a thin white dress, one slim hand caressing the bare branches as she went.

The video ended with a still image of Bourne Hall, lit by tendrils of sunrise and overlaid with the words: *Chateau Lafoute welcomes you to Bourne Hall for a grand tasting. From 1848 to the present day.*

Thankfully, it appeared Paloni had decided that his footage of the pseudo-Sir William, traipsing gaily around the gardens, was not quite in keeping with the rest of the montage.

The lights went up, and the guests looked around at each other in delighted anticipation.

Bertie cleared his throat and made as if to stand, but Ariane laid a quick hand on his, and rose to her feet.

"I, too, would like to give my thanks for your company here tonight," she said, smiling down the table. "But before we start the main tasting of the wines of Chateau Lafoute, I would like to propose a toast to a person dear to many who are here tonight. Without him, this tasting would not be possible, and all of us at Chateau Lafoute are much saddened to have lost such a friend and champion of our wines.

"Sir William was a man with a great, but very human, understanding of wine. He understood its need to be drunk, admired, not hidden away in the darkness. So please join me in a small tasting of some great wines that I am sure he would have wished to enjoy too, should he have been with us tonight. These wines come from the collection here at Bourne Hall, and though they are not from Chateau Lafoute, I am sure the selection will be a fitting tribute to a great man, sadly missed."

She nodded at Arthur, who looked around in some confusion. He had not been briefed on this part of the evening. Eventually, he noticed the dining room door had opened a crack, revealing the sight of Alf, jiggling from one foot to another, a silver trolley by his side.

On it stood four bottles from Sir William's prime collection: a '49 Margaux, a '61 Mouton-Rothschild, a '52 Pavie, and a '39 Latour. All in magnum.

As Arthur wheeled the trolley into the room, he noticed Bertie lean over to Ariane, his face tight with concern. "Darling, do you really think—"

"Wine is made for the human lips," replied Ariane, with some finality. Bertie retreated, brow furrowed as he looked around, trying to make sense of the change in proceedings.

Resnick, too, was looking rather put out, perhaps sensing that the night's carefully chosen line-up was now being upstaged. He hurried over as Arthur picked up the corkscrew with a certain amount of trepidation.

"Allow me, Arthur," he said. "These old bottles can be quite temperamental."

Arthur relinquished the corkscrew, with secret relief. He'd been witness over the years to a good number of old corks crumbling into their bottles, necessitating the hasty application of a fine sieve before drinking, and he had no wish for such a fiasco on his head tonight. Not with four of the world's foremost wine experts in the audience.

"Are you entirely certain about this, Mrs Lafoute?" said Resnick, pausing as he hovered over the wax seal of the first bottle. "I believe Sir William acquired these bottles in recent years, and although I cannot vouch for any exact valuation, of course, I can assure you that to open them all represents a significant loss to the collection, I hope you understand."

"I am definite in my choice," said Ariane coolly.

The critics were smiling at each other, like cats in a dairy. Like many wine writers, they themselves had very little personal wealth, and relied on the generosity of their hosts to acquire the depth and breadth of their knowledge and tasting notes, especially at the most expensive and rare end of the wine market.

"I hope you know what you're doing," muttered Paloni to Ariane, as he watched Resnick make his way around the table, pouring careful measures of the smooth caramel-brown liquid into each participant's glass.

Arthur's eyes followed every drop. To taste an old fine wine was more than just a pleasure; it was an experience, a slice of history, to imagine the air that these grapes had breathed, the lives of those—most of them now long gone—whose hands had brought these wines into being. And to taste not just any wines, but four titans of the Bordeaux region, side by side . . .

He wanted to kick Chef Maurice for not having got him an invite too.

As if by some sixth sense, the chef stopped in the middle of sniffing his glasses and turned around to look at him. Then he stood up, laid his napkin carefully on the table, and walked over to Arthur.

"*Mon ami*, please, take my place. You will appreciate this more, I am sure." He took the white waiter's cloth from Arthur's arm.

Arthur narrowed his eyes. "This is some kind of trick, isn't it? Have you spiked the wines with something?" His gaze was drawn upwards to the chandelier hanging heavily over the table. "Is something about to happen that I don't know about?"

"*Mon cher* Arthur! I make a most generous offer to my dear friend, and yet you—"

"All right, fine. Very, er, kind of you."

Arthur sat down in Chef Maurice's place and, with a last glance towards the chandelier above him, gingerly inched his chair forwards until he was sat with his nose over the four glasses.

The others barely noticed his arrival, so engrossed were they in the prizes before them, noses in glasses, taking the occasional little sips, accompanied by heady sighs. Bob Barker had his famous black spiral-bound notebook out, and Céleste Dauphine was tapping away at a slim electronic device held discreetly in her lap. There was the occasional murmur of astonishment, and various appreciative glasses were raised in Ariane's direction.

Arthur looked down at the wines before him. He couldn't shake the feeling that Chef Maurice had some hand in this, but to what end, he couldn't begin to fathom.

He'd watched Resnick carefully cut away the dusty wax seals and painstakingly ease out the old corks (which thankfully had all come out whole). So tampering was out of the question.

Was his friend trying to confuse their palates before the main event? But these were practised tasters, capable of making their way around the hundreds of wines present at a big tasting event.

From around the table, mutterings of 'majestic', 'hint of autumnal fruit', 'subdued but lively', '*incroyable*' and '*eindrucksvoll*' floated past.

Arthur finally gave in and picked up the first glass. Long-stewed berries, spice, and dark, earthy notes floated up his nostrils. On the palate, there was still the faintly lingering hint of red fruit, but mostly it was like drinking a very handsome, antique-filled, wood-panelled room. Utterly unforgettable.

He moved on to the next.

"Stunning," murmured Resnick, his usual sneer quite forgotten, replaced by a look of quiet reverence. "Each from a different vineyard and year, yet tied together by their shared histories. It's almost as if they're talking to each other through time . . . "

There were various nods from around the table, though Arthur caught Lady Margaret rolling her eyes heavenwards.

Only Bob Barker was wearing a slight frown.

"Mr Barker," said Ariane, raising her voice so that it

carried sweetly down the length of the table. "What is your opinion?"

"You want my honest opinion?" said the man, turning his gaze on his hostess.

"Nothing but honesty, please. After all"—Ariane gave a mischievous smile—"these are not made by *my* family. You may say anything you wish."

"Well, I've made my name by calling a spade a spade, and I'll be damned if I stop doing that today. Now, I apologise, Mrs Lafoute, I know this was a great gesture, very grand of you. But I have to break it to you—these four wines all taste exactly the same."

There were gasps from around the table. Arthur watched Bob Barker give Ariane a firm nod, his eyes not leaving her face. For a critic of his standing, to admit, in front of everyone, that he could not tell the difference between—

Wait a moment. Arthur quickly sniffed at his glasses, then tasted them, one by one, in random order.

He, too, rather prided himself on his palate. He'd even visited a taste lab once, for an article for the *England Observer*, to have his tongue and nasal receptors put to the test. They'd crowned him a super-taster (or -smeller, really), capable of discerning the most minute differences in a myriad of flavour profiles.

(This pronouncement had caused Chef Maurice, a sceptic when it came to anything involving microscopes, to start lacing Arthur's food with minuscule quantities of unexpected ingredients, in an effort to catch his friend out.

This had gone on for months, until a tarragon-and-clam chocolate pudding prompted Arthur to refuse to eat at Le Cochon Rouge anymore, until the flavour shenanigans ended.)

And, try as he might, as he went back and forth between the glasses, he had to agree that, somehow, Bob Barker was right. The wines weren't just spookily similar, they all tasted exactly the same, even given their differing ages. But how—?

Ariane looked down the table. "Mademoiselle Dauphine? Miss Fetters? Herr Herrmann? Do you agree?"

There was a pause, then a series of reluctant nods.

"I mean," said Miss Janet Fetters, "I wouldn't want to stake my life on it, but . . . "

"If you were offered a thousand pounds?" said Arthur.

"Yes, I'd say they all taste the same," she admitted.

Céleste nodded.

"I need no money," said Hunfrid Herrmann. "Same, they are all the same."

"Well, I think they're all marvellous," said Paloni loudly. The whole table shot him a look, and he sat back down again.

"But I don't understand. We all saw the bottles opened. How can—" started Arthur, but Chef Maurice had now made a sudden appearance at the head of the table, standing behind Ariane, tapping a corkscrew against one of the empty bottles.

"*Mesdames, messieurs.* If I may take your attention, I will now solve for you the mystery of these four bottles.

And in the same moment, we will together solve the crime of Sir William's murder. It is a story that starts with wine, and ends with greed. And it is also the story of what makes a true bottle of wine, and what this very truth must mean." A dramatic finger was raised.

Oh no, thought Arthur, he's at it again. He fished out his notebook, scribbled down a message, and dashed for the door.

It was time to call in reinforcements.

CHAPTER 17

PC Lucy stared down at the menu, her cheeks burning. Stupid, she was so stupid. To think that a guy like Patrick wouldn't have other girls on the go. It was true what they said about chefs—they weren't the steady sort. All the heat and passion of the kitchens, it addled their little—

"Penny for your thoughts?" said a familiar voice.

PC Lucy looked up and forced a smile. "Hi, guys. Perfect timing as usual."

Fred looked down at his wristwatch, confused. "But we're ten minutes late."

"Which counts as early in Sally time," replied PC Lucy, standing up to hug her sister.

Sally obliged with a peck to each cheek, then held her elder sibling back at arm's length. "You're not looking so good, Luce."

"Nice to see you too," said PC Lucy, sighing as she sat back down. "I'm fine, I just had a bit of a shock just now."

"Seen someone you need to arrest?" asked Sally with a giggle. She picked up the menu. "Oooh, look, babe," she said to Fred, "they've put the chicken dish back on the list!"

"She liked it so much," said Fred to PC Lucy, "she actually ventured into the kitchen and tried cooking it the other day."

"And?" To Lucy's recollection, her sister's culinary repertoire mostly consisted of toast *à la burnt scrapings*.

"Let's just say my cat left the house and didn't come back for three days." Fred planted a teasing kiss on Sally's cheek while she pouted.

PC Lucy rather liked Fred, the only one of her sister's boyfriends who had so far made it past the three-month mark. Perhaps because he was a little bit older than Sally's usual ripped-jeans, overly hair-gelled swains, it was possible to have an actual conversation with him, and his influence seemed to be having a beneficial effect on Sally's normally exuberant scattiness. Plus he seemed to genuinely care about her, and Sally for him—though PC Lucy still had suspicions that her sister's regard for Fred was not entirely hindered by the fact that he ran a multimillion-pound tech company. Still, PC Lucy had so far given Fred the tentative thumbs up.

"You know," said Sally, leaning close to PC Lucy's ear, "I think that guy over there is checking you out. There by the wall, with the dark hair and nerdy glasses. He's got nice shoulders, though, don't you think, Fred?"

"Not my type," replied Fred without looking up, as he perused the wine list.

"Will you stop that," chided PC Lucy, as her sister craned in her seat to try and get a better view.

"I'm allowed to *look*," said Sally. "Oh, how cute, now he's looking a bit embarrassed—"

"Fancy that."

"Have you seen him anywhere before?"

PC Lucy made a show of studying the starters with great concentration.

"So you *do* know him! Wait, not just that. You've been *out* with him, I can tell."

"How can you tell?" demanded PC Lucy.

Sally gave her an impish grin, and pushed her aside to get a better look. "I can't. But now you just told me."

"Bitch," muttered PC Lucy.

"He's not a bad looker, not that I'm any expert," said Fred, who evidently had decided he was not going to be able to escape the Patrick-watching game. "Looks like he works out a fair bit, your fellow."

"No, he doesn't," snapped PC Lucy. "And he's not my fellow. As evidenced by the fact he's clearly on a *date*, with that giraffe-legged supermodel who's making eyes at him."

"I don't know, she doesn't look that into him," said Sally, with the certainty of someone who'd been on dates with plenty of men she hadn't been particularly into, either. "So why haven't you introduced me to your guy?"

"Well, apart from the fact that he's *not my guy*, I've told you before, you do not get to meet anyone I'm dating."

"Oh, come on, Luce, that was all ages ago."

"What's this about?" said Fred.

"Back when I was in Kindergarten and she was in Form Two," said Sally in a sing-song voice, "she claims that she was going to pretend-marry Tommy Morris at lunchtime, but apparently I won him over with a potato stamp shaped like a rabbit and he pretend-married me instead."

"It's not funny," growled PC Lucy, as Fred started to smile. "And I'm not talking about play school. What about when I was nineteen, and you just had to go and nick Gary off me—"

"Oh, come on, that lasted, like, two weeks. And I did you a favour. I should have known any man *that* good-looking couldn't be straight," Sally added with a sigh.

"—and then there was that time I was just getting to know Paolo when you swooped in, completely fabricated some upcoming trip to Madrid to get him to give you Spanish lessons, then ended up taking a *very* suspicious siesta at his house!"

"Water under the bridge," said Sally, waving a hand. "It's not like you even liked any of those guys that much. Plus, I've got Fred now, so you don't need to worry." She planted a kiss on the tip of Fred's nose, who gazed back at her adoringly.

"You two make me sick," said PC Lucy, though she supposed she should be glad to see her sister so happy with a man apparently free of criminal records, drug habits and visible gang tattoos.

A waiter approached their table. "Miss Lucy Gavistone?"

"Yes?"

"You have a call at the desk."

"That's odd," she said, standing up. "Must be work. Though I wonder why they didn't call my phone . . . "

She followed the waiter over to reception and picked up the handset, while he hovered next to her impatiently, obviously worried about the hordes of callers currently trying to get through for a table.

"Miss Lucy?" It was Alf, sounding breathless.

"Yes? Has something happened at the restaurant? Why didn't you call my mobile?"

"Didn't have your number, miss. But they've got the phone book here, and Patrick said you'd be at Trattoria Bennucci—"

"What?!" The tables nearby looked around in alarm.

Alf was still chattering on.

"—Bourne Hall, and Arthur gave me a note and said to ring you. Said that chef's up to something again, and that you probably wouldn't want him, chef, I mean, to go arresting any murderers without proper instruction."

PC Lucy breathed in and counted to three. "Okay, I'll be right there."

She strode back over to her table. "Emergency at work," she said, giving her sister a brief hug and Fred a peck on the cheek. "Keep her out of mischief, will you?" she told him, as she flung on her coat and searched around for her bobble hat.

She forced herself not to look over to the back table where Patrick was no doubt whispering sweet nothings into the ear of that camel-eyed brunette.

Then she headed out into the cold night, ready to deal out merry hell to anyone who got in her way, and all chefs in particular.

Chef Maurice raised the empty bottle. "It is with much sadness that I must inform you that all four wines you have just tasted are, in fact, fakes."

There were gasps from around the table.

"Fakes?" said Bertie, looking stunned. "What does that even mean? How can you have a fake wine?"

Arthur noticed that the rest of the table—saving Lady Margaret, who seemed quite thrilled at this turn of events—did not look nearly as confused. In fact, they all looked rather grim.

"A good question, Monsieur Bertie," said Chef Maurice. "There are, so I am told, many different ways that one may manufacture a fake wine. Different levels of the art of forgery, one can say. The simplest is for one to take a completely genuine bottle, but to change the year on the label to another vintage of higher value. But this is not the case here, as it does not explain how these bottles taste entirely the same," he added, as Arthur opened his mouth to comment.

"Then," he continued, "there is the most grand, most daring type of fake wine. This is when only the glass itself of the bottle is the genuine item. The label, it is fake, of course. The cork, aged by chemical means. And the wine itself, it is not even always wine! A mixture of old wine, new wine, alcohol, colourings—a forger will use anything to allow the contents to look and smell as one imagines they should."

The whole table was now staring at the four empty bottles lined up in front of Chef Maurice.

"Aha! So I see you now ask, *how* fake are the wines you have tasted tonight? For this question, I turn to a man of much knowledge in these matters. I present to you Monsieur Mack, of the FBI of America."

The door swung open and a tall man in a grey suit, with neatly clipped ice-blond hair, stepped inside.

Alf, who had been standing just inside the door, gave a little yelp and ran behind a large potted plant.

"Monsieur Mack makes a speciality of the investigation into the fraud of wine. For many months, he has worked with Sir William and the Metropolitan Police Department of Art Fraud—*oui*, it is most pleasing, is it not, to see that wine is considered as art in this country—to gather the clues of a crime in action here in England. Sadly, a much greater crime took place before their work was complete.

"But one task that was finished was a scientific examination of these bottles in front of you. The labels scanned in tiny detail, and samples of the liquid drawn with a needle, he tells me. That these bottles look very real, that none of the experts here could give comment"—he nodded at

Resnick and the other critics—"is because they are. I mean to say, that the labels, the glass, all are original. But the wine inside, it was *not*.

"But how can this be? I then learn from Monsieur Mack that one may buy empty bottles of fine wines on the dark market, or steal them from restaurants after the true contents are consumed. They are then refilled to give the taste, the smell, of a fine old wine. This is what happened to these four bottles, manufactured by a master forger, most likely all at the same time."

"But how are these crooks getting away with this?" demanded Paloni. "One or two bottles, maybe, I can believe that, but once you opened enough of them—"

"Ah, but many collectors, they live to make their collections, not to drink them. The rich man or woman may buy so many fine bottles, yet never taste any. Especially in the case of the very rare, very expensive bottles. And so, we have a crime that so very often is not even detected in the first place."

"And wealthy folks don't exactly like to shout about it when they get stung," added Bob Barker.

"I knew that butler wasn't to be trusted!" said Lady Margaret. "Sneaking out of here with the real bottles, I'll wager, and replacing them with these abominable fakes. And then what he did to poor William. The man should hang!"

"*Non, madame*, I am afraid the blame cannot be put on Monsieur Gilles," said Chef Maurice. "But, you are correct when you say that the person who made the forgery of the wines is also the murderer of Sir William.

"And I can now say that this person sits with us, here. In this very room."

"Well, you're a piece of work, I'll tell you that."

A honeyed voice floated over Patrick's shoulder, and he turned around to find a blue-eyed, blond-haired young woman glaring down at him. With that particular expression, she bore a striking resemblance to PC Lucy, albeit a mildly underfed version with a slightly weaselly cast to her features. Still, from a distance, it would be easy to mistake the two of them . . .

"I'm Sally," she said, "and that's Fred, my boyfriend." She pointed over to the table so recently vacated by PC Lucy. "And you're the muttonhead who's just gone and upset my big sister. Don't think I don't see what's going on here."

She threw a scathing look at Isabella, who sat sipping on her Champagne with a look of mild amusement.

"It's not what it looks like," said Patrick quickly. "We're just friends. Colleagues, even."

"Of course, that bit's obvious," said Sally impatiently. "She's way out of your league."

Isabella gave her a gracious nod.

"But my sister's too ridiculous to see that. So now you've gone and made her think you don't give a fig about her."

"But . . . I thought . . . I mean, I didn't think she . . . " started Patrick.

"I know," sighed Sally, pulling up a chair to join them. "I saw your face just now. You're really into her, aren't you? So, luckily for you, I'm going to help you make things better. And not just because you're kind of cute." She leaned in. "You don't happen to have a brother, do you?"

"I heard that," called a voice from across the room.

Sally grinned. "I like to keep him on his toes," she whispered, blowing a kiss over to the indignant Fred.

"I don't think there's much I can do," said Patrick, glumly. "She's really mad at me. I saw that look of hers. I doubt anything I do is going to change that."

Sally looked at him. "Golly, you really don't know anything about women, do you?"

Chef Maurice swept his gaze around the table. The room was full of the sound of a dozen people holding their breath.

"First, we must consider those people who had often access to the wine cellar. *Oui*, there was Monsieur Gilles, but it was not only him. Many of you here came often to the Hall, and as trusted visitors were allowed to go and admire the cellar, perhaps even left alone there."

"But how would anyone be able to take away the bottles without Sir William noticing?" said Arthur.

"Ah, that comes later, *mon ami*. But first, we know Sir William began to hold suspicions. He sends bottles to London, under the trust of Monsieur Gilles, to have them examined. He seeks to make a new catalogue of his collection.

"And so, our criminal feels the net closing around. The investigation of Sir William must be stopped before he discovers too much."

Arthur looked around the table, scrutinising each guest in turn. The critics were looking uncomfortable, as if they'd wandered accidentally into a blazing family row. Of the others, all looked shocked, but none more worried or haunted than the other. Apart from perhaps Ariane, who continued to wear a tight smile.

He also saw Chef Maurice running a piercing glare over each face: Paloni, Bertie, Ariane, Resnick, Lady Margaret, and then back again. A sinking feeling hit him.

Maurice didn't know who it was. Or if he did, he didn't have a shred of proof. Perhaps he thought the pressure of an audience, plus the FBI chap—whose sudden appearance Arthur still didn't quite understand—would scare the perpetrator into standing up and committing a swan song, a damning confession. Or at least into trying to make a run for it.

"I see you look around," said Chef Maurice finally. "You ask, is it he, is it she? Who can be responsible? But, again, I give thanks to Monsieur Mack. From the work of him and his *collègues*, we need not to study the face of our neighbours. Because we have it here, clear for all to see . . . "

Chef Maurice picked up the remote control from beside Ariane's motionless hand and pressed a button. The picture of Bourne Hall was replaced by grainy footage of

247

the interior of the wine cellar, shot from high up in one corner.

A hidden camera! thought Arthur. All this time . . .

The rolling shot showed Sir William's back as he stood before a set of shelves, holding a bottle in one hand and carefully wiping down its sides with a polishing cloth.

From this angle, Arthur noticed that Sir William had a burgeoning bald spot on the top of his head that Arthur had never noticed before. He shook himself. Now was not the time for such thoughts.

In the corner of the screen, a pair of black patent leather shoes appeared from behind the wine crates. They stepped towards Sir William with quiet, deadly purpose—

"Enough!" shouted a strangled voice. A figure jumped up from the table and started tearing madly at the hanging screen. Then he stood panting, staring at them all, as the screen ribboned down behind him onto the floor.

"Ah, *monsieur*," said Chef Maurice. "You do not wish that I continue this film?"

He smiled at the figure at the front of the room, flickering in the light of the still-rolling projector. It was Charles Resnick.

CHAPTER 18

The kitchens of Bourne Hall had run out of chairs, even with the departure of many of the guests. The four wine critics had headed back to London to write up their impressions of the startling evening, and FBI Agent Mack had accompanied Charles Resnick away in a car sent by the Metropolitan Police Art Fraud department. Everyone else had retired to the kitchens in search of a comforting cup of tea, and Mrs Bates currently had three kettles on the boil. Waffles weaved in and out of the many legs around the table, biding her time until she could catch the milk jug unawares.

Arthur was the first to voice his objections.

"But that was *cheating*! If you knew there was a CCTV camera all along—"

"Ah, but, *mon ami*, you do not see—"

"—and, worse still, how could our own police have missed it in the first place?" Arthur turned to PC Lucy, who had arrived towards the end of the night's proceedings, just in time to witness Resnick's monumental breakdown.

"There *was* no CCTV," said PC Lucy hotly. "We checked all over. Double-checked, triple-checked, even."

"Then how—"

"Think, *mon ami*," said Chef Maurice, who was sat at the end of the table with Hamilton in his lap.

Once again, Arthur fought the urge to thump his friend on the top of his conceited head.

"It was a fake video, it must have been," said PC Lucy. "The quality was far too good, for one. And that wasn't Sir William, was it?"

"Aha!" said Chef Maurice, looking pleased.

"I have to admit my team might have had a hand in that," said Paloni, unleashing a dazzling smile in PC Lucy's direction. "After Mr Maurice here talked me into his little scheme."

"Damnation, so *that's* what you were up to," said Arthur, slapping the table and sending a plate of biscuits flying. "The actor chap you had wandering around the grounds . . ."

Paloni nodded. "I was sure glad that Resnick fella tore down the screen at that point. Else you'd have seen that those black leather shoes were me, and I sure as hell don't look a thing like him. You might have even thought to arrest me," he added, with a wink at PC Lucy, who narrowed her eyes at him.

"I still don't get it," said Bertie, who was sharing a chair with Ariane, one arm around her waist. "So he was stealing wine from Uncle William's cellar and replacing them with fakes? And what, selling the real bottles on after?"

"*Non, non*, even better than that. There were no real bottles to start with. Monsieur Resnick would buy empty bottles, and even sometimes manufacture the labels himself. Then he would fill them and sell them to collectors. Sometimes even at his own auctions. He would claim to have bought them from those secretly wishing to cash in their cellars, but who did not want to have it known. And in this way, he never had need to reveal his sources."

"And none of his clients ever suspected? Apart from Sir William?" said Arthur.

"Many didn't. Or perhaps they chose to stay silent," said Chef Maurice. "But there was one collector in America who became suspicious, which is how Monsieur Mack became involved. He tells me that most of the wines found to be fake could be traced back to Monsieur Resnick and his company. But they needed to find a collector in Britain to also make a case, so that Monsieur Resnick could be put on trial here too. It was at this time that Sir William first contacted the police in London. It had taken him much time to have suspicions of someone he had known and trusted for so long . . . "

"But how did Resnick find out about the Met investigation?" said Arthur.

Chef Maurice shrugged. "Monsieur Resnick will tell the police, I am sure. It is possible he realised the suspicions when he saw the yellow stickers that Sir William and Monsieur Mack used to mark those bottles that they had doubts on.

"But for me, I think Sir William was a gentleman, to the very end. Remember, he spoke to Monsieur Resnick in his office, earlier that day of the tasting. It is my thought that he told Monsieur Resnick of the investigation, to give him the sporting chance, as you say, to go himself to the police. Monsieur Resnick, he pretends to agree, begs to stay for the dinner to keep up appearances, but in truth, he has other plans. He cuts the phone line, so that there is no chance for Sir William to ring to the police, and then that evening, he takes his steps to silence him altogether."

"An evil man," said Ariane with a shiver.

"So how does this Agent Mack fellow fit in all this?" said Arthur. "What was he doing down at Le Cochon Rouge on the night of the murder?"

"He was waiting, he tells me, for a call from Monsieur Gilles who, under Sir William's instruction, had prepared further important bottles to give to Monsieur Mack to take to London for investigation. But with the phone lines cut, Monsieur Gilles had no way to contact him. So, after waiting for long, Monsieur Mack telephones to his *supérieurs*, who instruct him to go to Bourne Hall, to collect the wines."

"And get chased away by you and your frying pan," said Arthur.

Chef Maurice coughed. "That was, I think, unfortunate."

"But how did you figure out who he actually was? And get him here tonight?"

"Ah, his role, I had made a guess of this when we followed him to the Department of Art Fraud in London.

Remember, where the Superintendent was most rude to us, and insisted that no such man had come inside?

"And then, just last night, I find this man in the restaurant's cellar! He searches, he tells me, within the bottles Sir William left there, as he cannot return to Bourne Hall, now with Monsieur Bertie in residence and Monsieur Gilles not there."

"Speaking of Gilles, what's happened to that fellow anyway? Resnick didn't, um, deal with him too, did he?"

"*Non.* Agent Mack did not want to take chances. He did not know if Monsieur Resnick knew of how Monsieur Gilles had assisted Sir William with the investigation. So he sends him to hide in a bed and breakfast in Brighton, he tells me."

"So really, solving this case was all this Mack fellow's doing then?"

"Not at all!" said Chef Maurice, bristling. "*Oui*, it was Monsieur Mack who supplied the fine details, but I had already many suspicions of Monsieur Resnick, and of the existence of the fake wines. Much before the help of Monsieur Mack."

"Codswallop," said Arthur. "I don't believe you."

"Here, I show you." Chef Maurice picked up a copy of the list of Lafoute vintages that would have been served that night. "Madame Lafoute, *regarde*. Think, think deeply, about the history of your family, of the chateau, and tell me what you see."

Ariane bit her lip and ran her eyes up and down the list. After a long silence, she gave a sudden gasp. "*Imbecile*, I am! My *grand-mère*, she would be ashamed of me not to see this. A 1928 magnum? *C'est ridicule!* Monsieur Manchot, you are magnificent."

"He is?" said Arthur.

"Madame Ariane is too kind," said Chef Maurice, but he looked excessively pleased with himself, as he pulled out the wine book he'd borrowed off Alf again.

"You still do not see, *mon ami*? Listen to this. 'Chateau Lafoute, founded in 1779, was long-time considered one of the more minor Bordeaux chateaux until its rise to prominence in the wake of the Second World War, with a later surge of interest in the 1980s when Bob Barker, renowned American wine critic, anointed the 1986 vintage with a perfect 314 out of 314.'"

Chef Maurice closed the book. "So you see? A rise to prominence *after the Second World War*. Remember, to produce the magnum size of bottle was an expensive task, only done by the bigger chateaux. For Chateau Lafoute to have produced magnums in 1928, pffffft! *Impossible!*"

"So Resnick slipped up?" said Arthur. "He went and faked a wine that didn't actually exist?"

Chef Maurice nodded. "He sold it to Sir William many years ago, not expecting that Sir William would develop a great interest in the wines of Chateau Lafoute. After all, if Monsieur Bertie here had not met *la belle* Ariane . . . "

"So that was all?" pressed Arthur. "Just one fake wine? That's *all* you had to go on?"

"*Non, non*, my suspicions of Monsieur Resnick, they had been there from the very start."

"Oh, come on now."

"Ah, but think. That evening when we sat in the drawing room, which of the guests had the most reason to go upstairs? To have the chance to enter the secret passageway and descend to the cellar?"

Chef Maurice reached down and, with one hand, lifted up a grumpy-looking Waffles, who had yet to score a saucer of milk. "The man, of course, who found himself covered in the hair of a cat!"

Waffles meowed plaintively, and Chef Maurice placed her back down onto the warm tiles.

"Remember, Monsieur Resnick had been many times to this house. He would surely know that the cat would ruin his clothes if she came too close. Yet he lets her sit in his lap, perhaps entices her even—remember the jar of the potted mackerel in his room?—to have an excuse to go upstairs when Sir William was down in the cellar. So he goes to the bookcase, which he has discovered on a visit before, goes down the stairs, makes certain Sir William is alone, then he makes his move . . . "

"A risky endeavour," said Arthur.

"He planned it pretty well, though," said PC Lucy, hands cupped around a mug of tea. "The business with the broken storeroom window, if he hadn't had the bad luck that it snowed heavily that evening, we might have taken the whole outside burglary idea more seriously. It was only the lack of footprints that focussed our attentions on the guests themselves."

"So do you think they'll be able to trace all the fakes back to Resnick?" said Arthur.

"It looks likely," said PC Lucy. "I had a quick chat with Agent Mack. He seems to have got hold of Sir William's old cellar book. Says it's a key piece of evidence."

"So that was what Gilles handed over to him, that day in London," said Arthur.

Chef Maurice nodded.

"What will happen to Charles now?" said Bertie.

"He'll stand trial for murder, of course," said PC Lucy. "And as for the wine forgery, it sounds like they have a pretty tight case. Frankly, his career was over the minute those bigwig critics tasted those fakes, and he knows it. They can't *not* write about it, because the other three will rat them out if they don't. So everyone is bound to hear all about this."

"So Resnick pretty much invited the world's four biggest wine critics to his own downfall," said Arthur. "Bit of a mistake, I'll say."

"*Non, non,*" said Chef Maurice, dropping three sugars into his teacup. "His mistake, I think, was for him to commit a crime on a night that I, Maurice Manchot, was present."

There was a resounding groan from all around the table.

CHAPTER 19

It was the Saturday morning, the week after. Fluffy white smoke trailed out of the chimney of The Goat and Gavotte, a friendly pub in the nearby village of Little Bottom.

Patrick walked, with some trepidation, down the frosty path towards the front door, where a blond head under a pink knitted hat was waiting for him.

"Finally! It's freezing out here, you know." Sally looked him up and down with a critical eye. "Good, you've shaved. That shows that you care. And you brought flowers"— she leaned in closer to inspect the bunch of roses in his hand— "hmmm, not very imaginative, but fairly swanky. Not bad at all, I had you down as the yellow carnation type." She wrinkled her nose at this thought. "Right, you better get in there, or I'm going to start getting calls asking where I am. Oh, and take this."

She shoved a box of chocolates, topped by a big satin bow, into his hands. This was followed by a piece of lined paper.

"That's what you're going to say."

Patrick looked over his script. It said, in essence, everything he had been planning to say anyway. That he was sorry for trying to make Lucy jealous, it had all been a stupid mistake, and she was the only girl he had eyes for. Except that Sally, a recipient of many such speeches in her lifetime and so able to select from the choicest of available phrasings, had wrapped the whole thing up in verbal flowers, rainbows, kittens and everything else an actual man would never say in a million years.

This was pure dating gold.

"Now, go get her, chef boy." Sally crossed her arms. "And don't screw it up. Else you'll have me to deal with."

Patrick had no desire to find out what exactly this entailed. Sally, underneath her girly-girl exterior, was turning out to be every bit as ferocious as her older sister.

He found PC Lucy sitting in a snug alcove by the pub's fireplace, wearing a soft green turtleneck jumper and jeans. Patrick thought he'd never seen her looking so good.

She didn't appear particularly surprised to see him.

"I thought she'd pull something like this," she said. "You usually can't get that girl out of bed before two on a weekend, not even using a first-class ticket to Paris. I saw some poor guy try. He ended up having to go by himself."

"Er, may I?" Patrick waved at the seat opposite her. PC Lucy shrugged.

He sat down and squared his shoulders. "Lucy. I know I well and truly messed up. I should have never doubted—"

"Wait." She held out her hand. "Give me the piece of paper."

Sheepishly, Patrick reached into his pocket and handed over Sally's instructions. "How did you know—"

"Oh, she's great at these. She even writes Fred's apologies to her, whenever he does something that pisses her off. I told her she should set up a speechwriting business."

She looked over the lines, then nodded.

"Okay, so tell me what you were *actually* going to say."

"Er. I'm sorry about, uh, following you to the restaurant the other night. And, uh, sorry for thinking you were dating that other guy. Though to be absolutely fair, Alf is a little bit to blame for that too. I thought about bringing him along. He wanted to apologise himself, but Sally said that wasn't a good idea"—PC Lucy gave him another nod—"so I didn't. And uh, sorry about the whole Isabella thing."

"So she has a name, does she?" said PC Lucy, with a certain amount of venom in her voice.

"Er. Yes?" Patrick couldn't help being a little surprised. "So, you mean, it worked? You *were* jealous?"

"Ugh, I knew I shouldn't have let you improvise!" PC Lucy shook her head. "Of course I was! Who wouldn't be jealous?"

"Well . . . In all honesty, I've always thought she looks a bit like a horse. She's got that horsey type of nose, and she's . . . well, a bit bony looking. But, I mean, she was the only girl I could think of who's even half as beautiful as you. Um, not that it's all about looks, of course. She's not funny like you are. Or as scary. In a good way, I mean. Though I did see her once pin a commis chef to the door with his jacket and a pair of fish skewers, because he burnt ten litres of veal stock . . . "

PC Lucy was now looking at him with a strange expression.

"Did my sister put you up to that, too?"

"Er, up to what?"

"That stuff you just said, about me being twice as . . . pretty . . . "

"No. That just . . . came out. Was it okay?"

She looked at him, that strange expression still on her face. "It'll do. For the moment. And I'd like my chocolates now, please."

Patrick pulled out the box Sally had given him.

"How did you—"

"Oh, it's another part of her standard procedure." PC Lucy lifted up the lid. "Oh good, they've brought back the sea salt caramels."

"I can make you those, if you like them." He essayed a tentative grin. "So, um, are we good?"

"After you called me more beautiful than that leggy giraffe girl? Yeah, I think we'll be fine." For the first time that morning, she smiled. Her fingers reached for his own. "Maybe even more than fine. I'm sorry I didn't tell you about Sally earlier. Would have saved you all that effort going shopping. Though I like the new coat, by the way."

Their make-up kiss was interrupted by the frantic tapping on the window pane next to them. Sally's face appeared, followed by a big thumbs up.

PC Lucy pulled the blind down.

"Wait. Sally didn't make a move on you, did she?"

"Nope. She did ask me how much chefs earned—I think she kind of lost interest after that. She's not my type anyway. She's too . . . fluffy." He cupped her hands in his own. "Are you free tomorrow evening? So I can take you out and make it up to you?"

"Will I have to look at any naked men?"

"Well, I can only guarantee one . . . "

PC Lucy slapped his hands away, rolled her eyes, and went to get them drinks

Well, it was bound to work one day . . .

CHAPTER 20

It was the second official meeting of the Cochon Rouge Wine Appreciation Society. Their numbers had been augmented this evening by the presence of PC Lucy, holding Patrick's hand under the table, and Agent Mack.

The FBI agent was sat between Chef Maurice and Arthur, due to the fact that Alf was still refusing to be within a one-foot radius of him, and Patrick surreptitiously manoeuvring his newly acquired girlfriend into a seat where she only had a partial view of Agent Mack's chiselled jawline.

In honour of the upcoming festive period, they opened proceedings with a round of big glasses of mulled wine, made by Alf to Chef Maurice's special recipe.

"This is very, very good," said Arthur, nodding at Alf. "Even better than usual. What wine are you using as the base nowadays?"

"I thought people might ask. Tada!" Alf pulled a great big bottle up from under the table. It was a jeroboam, four times the size of a normal wine bottle. The label was smudged and discoloured, but still managed to proclaim itself to be the '66 vintage from one of Burgundy's most esteemed vineyards.

"Don't worry," added Alf, as he saw their faces. "I was watching Mr Mack down in our cellar earlier"—despite his terror of the FBI agent, Alf had been gagging to see a real federal wine inspection in action—"when he was going through the wines Sir William left here, and he said this one was definitely a fake."

The table turned to Agent Mack.

"I thought I said it was most likely a fake ... " he hedged.

"How likely a fake?" asked Chef Maurice. Everyone held their breath. They all knew Sir William had bequeathed the chef the entire contents of that particular wine rack.

Agent Mack appeared to consider his chances. "Definitely. Hundred percent a fake. But, to help with the case, if you don't mind, I think I'll take that bottle with me ... "

He prised the giant bottle out of Alf's white-knuckled grip.

Chef Maurice stared reflectively at his glass. "*Bon*. Wine is, after all, made to be drunk." He downed the glass's contents.

They all agreed afterwards it was the best mulled wine they'd ever tasted.

J.A. Lang is a British mystery author. She lives in Oxford, England, with her husband, an excessive number of cookbooks, and a sourdough starter named Bob.

Want more Chef Maurice?

To receive email notification when the next Chef Maurice mystery is released, as well as news about future book releases by J.A. Lang, subscribe to the newsletter at:

www.jalang.net/newsletter

CPSIA information can be obtained at www.ICGtesting.com
Printed in the USA
LVOW07s1814260216

476854LV00008B/481/P